NEW CENTURY READERS

Flour Babies

Anne Fine

Notes: Esther Menon

Edinburgh Gate
Harlow, Essex

Pearson Education Limited
Edinburgh Gate
Harlow
Essex
CM20 2JE
England

ISBN 978-0-582-43452-3

Printed in China
GCC/14

Designed and packaged by McLean Press Ltd
Cover illustration by Stephanie Axtell

Contents

Introduction

About the author

Born in Leicester, Anne Fine worked as a teacher and an information officer for Oxfam, before marrying and having two daughters. She has lived in Canada, the United States and Britain. Anne began writing after having her first child – she found herself stuck in a high-rise flat in a snow storm with her small baby and could not get to a library to find something fresh to read. So she sat down and started to write.

She did not find immediate success with her first novel, *The Summer House Loon*, which was not published until 1975, three years after she wrote it, when it was runner-up in the Guardian-Kestrel competition. Since then she has written numerous novels, including *Goggle-Eyes*, which won the Carnegie Medal and Guardian's Fiction Award, and *Flour Babies* which also won the Carnegie Medal and the Whitbread Prize. Her book, *Madame Doubtfire* was made into a very successful film, starring Robin Williams and Sally Field.

Why does she choose the subjects she does? Anne Fine says she writes 'the book you would most like to read, but no one has bothered to write for you'. She chooses subjects that are sometimes seen as quite difficult or sophisticated for children. But she argues: children may lack power and experience, but they do not lack intelligence. 'Children live in the real world.'

Anne does not write down to children. As you will see, when you read *Flour Babies*, Anne, like many a parent, has a good understanding of how difficult the task of being a parent can be and how frustrating and difficult life can be when you are a child, especially in periods of change. Her books are full of realism, and her characters do not have an easy time. They have to learn to cope with events not of their choosing and often have to adapt to changed circumstances. However, as she says, 'I wouldn't want a child to finish one of my books and feel absolutely hopeless and miserable. So, though I might not have a 'happy ending', I always like to offer some strong hope for the future, some way of going forward.'

Anne has now written a great number of books for children, as well as three novels for adults, and her books have been translated all over the world. But she still takes a long time to get her novels exactly right: 'I … rub out constantly. My first pages look disgusting, filthy, quite unreadable. They'd send a teacher's hair grey. I write a sentence, fret about every word, twist it all round, rewrite it, rub it out … I'll pore over the same paragraph for three days.' This is something she never dreamt she would have to do when she was at school: her idea then was to finish everything as quickly as she possibly could.

Anne is never worried about using long words though, since she strongly believes that if the book is interesting, readers will be happy to push on and learn more through their reading.

Ever since she was a child one thing has not changed: all her life she has always read and she still reads and reads and reads: 'I read in the bath, in bed, even while I'm walking the dog – I have a sort of second sight for messes on the pavement. I know that, if I hadn't been a reader, I would never have been a writer … The best advice for a would-be writer is: Read, read, read.'

Setting the scene

The two main settings of *Flour Babies* are familiar to most of us: school and home. Our main characters are in class 4C and we follow their reactions to a new project they undertake as part of their contribution to the school Science Fair. At the opening of the book, the class greet their project options with cries of 'Boring!',

'It isn't fair, sir!,' yet how differently students react and change during the three-week project, as they look after bags of flour to learn about the responsibilities of being a parent! The action moves between the realistic settings of school, home and the places where the students socialise.

Anne Fine is concerned about the growing trend for teenage pregnancy in the 1990s in western society and the responsibilities that go with it. She looks at the difficulties and pleasures of being a teenager, and the process of growing into a deeper understanding of oneself and others.

Main character and summary

The main character in the novel is Simon Martin, a big clumsy boy who, his form teacher says, 'goes about behaving like a half-wit'. He often finds himself in trouble, sent out of assembly and in detention. Even there he cannot resist causing problems, by forgetting equipment, noisily borrowing some, noisily drumming his pencil in the silence, pulling faces … so if he occasionally falls asleep in detention instead of doing his work, the teacher does not say anything, but sighs with relief.

The project of looking after the flour-bag babies seems to change Simon: the teachers cannot quite believe what they are seeing, and his friends think he has lost his sanity. Caring for this imaginary baby makes Simon reflect on his own childhood and the fact that his own father shirked this responsibility and left him and his mother. It seems to bring into focus issues about his father that have been worrying him for years, for his mother won't speak about what happened. By the end of the three-week period, he realises the huge responsibility of looking after another life, but also the pleasure and companionship that go with it. He begins to appreciate what his mother has done for him and, perhaps also, the reasons why his father was not able to do so.

In portraying the varying characters in 4C and their contrasting reactions to the flour babies' project Anne Fine shows the different levels of maturity and understanding of the boys in the class: Sajid whose business skills are put into practice in making money out of looking after other people's flour babies; Gwyn Phillips who can't be bothered to write out his baby book so instead copies Wayne Driscoll's; Wayne who thinks about his mixed-race background and Robin Foster who gets so frustrated he kicks his flour baby into the canal.

Main themes

Flour Babies deals with a number of important themes, the most obvious being parenthood and responsibility. The boys have to keep their flour babies clean and dry and ensure that they are looked after at all times of the day and night, a responsibility that reduces 4C to silence when they first hear it. Through this theme we are able to compare and contrast the boys' reactions to this responsibility. It is clear that they are far from ready to take on such a role in real life, though we can also see that some have the potential to be good parents. Simon's father, we also see, was obviously young when he had Simon, and lacked the maturity to be able to fulfil his responsibilities.

The theme of growing up is developed as some of the students are described playing roles that they might aspire to in real life, for example Sajid, who starts his own profitable business babysitting other people's flour babies. Fine shows us by the end of the novel that growing up is about coming to an understanding of ourselves and others, as Simon begins to understand his father's actions, appreciate his mother's, and see a bit of both his parents in himself.

Early in the novel, Mr Cartright wonders 'Why had schools been invented, for heaven's sake?' The nature and purpose of education is a central theme of the book. The characters in 4C have been

4

labelled by some of the teachers as not worth educating. Yet the novel explores education in a wider sense, and focuses on the boys' education both inside and outside the classroom. Fine invites us to compare the teachers in the novel: the stern Mr Cartright who, frustrated by their difficulties in reading, seems to have dismissed the boys in his class; the more modern Dr Feltham who appears willing to give everyone an equal chance to succeed, and Miss Arnott who enjoys the personalities and pranks of her students, despite the frequent headaches they give her.

The themes addressed in *Flour Babies* are common to many of Anne Fine's books. Her novels frequently explore young people's struggles to move towards personal identity; the weaknesses of adults and children's ability to grow up quickly and support the adults around them

Flour Babies is a novel rooted in real life. While the students have to *imagine* their bags of flour as real babies, the setting, characters and life experiences of these characters are very real. Fine addresses many issues that are highly relevant to both young people and adults today. While she considers the serious matters of parenthood, responsibilities and education, these are viewed through the eyes of young people who are developing their skills of personal choice and empathy with others. We are not left with a moralising lecture, but a novel which is thought-provoking and relevant, leaving readers to come to their own personal decisions.

Flour Babies

Notes for Chapter 1

Anne Fine uses two methods at the beginning of *Flour Babies* to develop the readers' curiosity. The novel opens in the middle of a lesson, which means we need to work at placing ourselves in this situation and pick up clues without the help of an introductory description. Secondly, in line two, Mr Cartright is talking about 'it', which is puzzling for the reader. This makes us want to read on to find out what 'it' is.

What do you think?

During the first chapter, Fine allows you to see the point of view of the teacher and his perceptions of his class. You are introduced to a familiar situation from two points of view; your own as students, and the teacher's. As you witness Mr Cartright's viewpoint, consider the reasons for the behaviour of the class.

Questions

1. Do you think Mr Cartright is a good teacher? What do you like about him and where do you see problems in his teaching methods?
2. List the words and phrases in this chapter which suggest that these students are difficult and restless. Pick three that you think best help you to imagine the class.
3. If you were teaching 4C what classroom rules would you set at the beginning of term? Decide on seven rules. Think carefully about the words you would use to write them out for the class.

Further activity

Start to make a list of the familiar phrases that teachers or parents use. You will find several in Mr Cartright's speech in this chapter, for example: 'I'll be delighted to go over it again in your break-time' and 'I don't remember anyone telling you this lesson was over'. Turn your list into a poem entitled *Parents' sayings* or *Teachers' sayings*. You might like to perform it to the class or make a poster poem on sugar paper incorporating ideas from other people in your class.

Chapter 1

Mr Cartright swung his legs to and fro under the desk, and raised his voice over the waves of bad-tempered muttering.

'Don't worry if you feel you can't give this your full attention now, 4C,' he said to his new class. 'I'll be delighted to go over it again in your break-time.'

Some of them visibly made a bit of an effort. A few pens were pulled out of a few mouths. One or two of the boys swivelled their heads back from the riveting sight of the janitor painting large white numbers on the dustbins. But, on the whole, the improvement was pitiful. Half of them looked as if they'd left their brains at home. The other half looked as if they didn't have any.

This year's 4C. What a shower! Mr Cartright knew most of them well enough already – the Sads and the Bads, the ones who had been despaired of most loudly and often in the staffroom over the last couple of years. Anyone halfway normal (these were called the Lads) had been bagged, as usual, by Mr King or Mr Henderson. And Dr Feltham always snaffled up the Boffins. So far, no one had ever fetched up in 4C by accident.

The only boy new to the school – what was his name, Martin Simon? – was sitting reading quietly at the back. Mr Cartright cheered up a bit. That was a start, then. One of them could read. He must have had worse classes in his time.

'Buck up,' he told them. 'This shouldn't take all day. I'll

run through the choices one last time, and then you'll have to vote. You can carry on eating your voting paper, George Spalder, but I'm not giving you another. Now pay attention, everyone.'

Shifting his vast bottom round, he tapped the blackboard on which, five minutes earlier, he'd chalked up the options Dr Feltham had given 4C for their contribution to the school Science Fair,

> textiles
> nutrition
> domestic economy
> child development
> consumer studies

reciting them aloud again, for those who had trouble with reading.

A swell of grumbling rose over the fidgets and whispers and shuffling feet, and the creak of chairs being tipped back dangerously on two of their four legs.

'It isn't fair, sir.'

'Boring!'

'You can't call that lot Science. It's not right.'

'I don't even know what half of them *mean*.'

To oblige Russ Mould, Mr Cartright read them off again, this time translating as he went along.

> sewing
> food
> housekeeping
> babies and so forth
> thrift

Russ Mould was as baffled as ever.

'Frift? What's frift?'

Mr Cartright chose to ignore him.

'For God's sake, 4C,' he said. 'Pull yourselves together. I know most of you have the boredom thresholds of brain-damaged gnats, but surely one of these topics must interest you more than the others. Whichever it is, copy it down on the paper. And do try to get the letters more or less in the right order, Russ Mould, so I can read it. I'm coming round now to collect them.'

Another mutinous wave rose up to greet him.

'Stupid!'

'Just trying to pick on us ...'

'Sewing! Housekeeping!'

'Excuse me. We're Table 14 in the Science Fair. Come and look at our nice sewed-on buttons.'

'Dead interesting. Oh, yes!'

'I bet you've never seen a sewed-on button before.'

'What's the point in doing things if *anyone* can do them?'

'Frift!'

It was Sajid Mahmoud who voiced the general complaint in the most coherent fashion.

'It isn't fair. They're not *real* Science, are they? None of them. Why can't we do the exploding custard tins?'

Instantly, it was as if the whole lot of them had been let out of a cage.

'Yes! They were great!'

'Dead brilliant.'

11

'Hooper's brother nearly burned his hand off.'

'Chop lost an eyebrow.'

'Grew back different.'

Rick Tullis was leaning so far over his desk, it was likely to topple over.

'Or making soap, sir!'

'Yes! The soap factory!'

'Fuller ate his lump for a dare.'

'Sick *eight times*.'

'We had a good laugh.'

'Should have seen his face. Pale as a maggot!' At this, Philip Brewster unleashed a fresh hue and cry round the room.

'Yes! Maggots!'

'Maggot farm!'

'Yes! Why can't we do the maggot farm?'

'There was one last year. And the year before.'

'My mum wouldn't even *look* at it. She said it was disgusting.'

'That bully Fletcher was put in charge of running it.'

'He practically had the maggots *trained* by the last day!'

Mr Cartright shook his head. It saddened him to have to dampen enthusiasm in any educational sphere. But facts are facts, especially in a school.

'May I invade your privacy for a moment, Sajid, to ask if you happened to pass the Physics exam at the end of last term?'

Sajid scowled horribly.

'No, I didn't, sir.'

'And you, Rick. Did you pass Chemistry?'

Rick Tullis laughed. And so did everyone who'd been in last year's Chemistry class along with Rick Tullis.

Mr Cartright turned to Philip, who was still bright-eyed at the thought of running the Maggot Farm.

'Philip? Any luck with Biology?' Philip's expression soured.

'I didn't even bother to come in and take it, sir. No point.'

Mr Cartright sighed.

'Well, there you have it in a nutshell, I'm afraid, 4C. No one is here by accident.'

At the back, suddenly, the new boy, Martin Simon, spoke up for the first time.

'I think I might be, sir.'

But Mr Cartright, in full flow, ignored the interruption.

'And therein lies the explanation of why, sadly, this class can't do the Exploding Custard Tins. In the absence of total confidence in your skills and commitment, Dr Feltham has entrusted us only with nice, safe and easy topics. Exploding Custard Tins have been reserved for those who passed Physics at the end of last year.'

His eye roved over eighteen sullen faces and one rather intrigued one.

'Did *anyone* here pass Physics?'

The new boy raised his hand. Otherwise, no one stirred. And since Martin Simon was pretty well out of everyone's line of sight, in the back row, Mr Cartright chose not to let his one waving arm detract from the dramatics of the occasion.

'Anyone pass Chemistry?'

Again, Martin Simon's hand shot up in the air, to be totally ignored by Mr Cartright. Otherwise, nothing much happened.

'Goodbye, Soap Factory,' Mr Cartright said. 'How was our record in Biology? Anyone have any luck there?'

Martin Simon's arm waved, a lone reed over the silt of the rest of 4C's academic hopes. For the third time, Mr Cartright pretended not to see it.

'So,' he said flatly. 'No Maggot Farm for us.'

He spread his huge chalky hands.

'You can't say you weren't warned,' he told them. 'I fetch my coffee from the staffroom. I have ears. Mr Spencer, Mr Harris, Mr Dupasque, Miss Arnott. They all said it, more than once. *"I've warned them over and over,"* they all said. *"If they don't work, they'll end up in 4C."* And here you are.

'You can't help it if you're stupid,' George Spalder argued.

'If you were stupid enough to be in 4C, you'd be on a life-support system,' said Mr Cartright tartly.

'So what are we doing here?'

Mr Cartright turned biblical.

'You're reaping as ye sowed. And, speaking of sewing, will you please get on and vote. What's it to be? Textiles, nutrition, domestic economy, child development or consumer studies?'

'I'm not voting for none of them,' said Gwyn Phillips. 'They're all stupid.'

Having a sneaking sympathy for this point of view, Mr Cartright said nothing. But when George Spalder added,

'Girls' things, that's what they are!' he felt obliged to put 4C right.

'Don't kid yourselves. While you lot are sitting here grumbling, girls all over the country are making soap, farming maggots and exploding custard tins. They're studying Chemistry, Biology and Physics. To the Victor the Spoils now. And they passed exams.'

Then, tiring suddenly of the whole boiling, he started striding up and down the rows of desks, chivvying them into voting. 'Get *on* with it, Robin Foster. Hurry up, Rick. What difference is it going to make to you? According to Miss Arnott, you hardly ever come to school anyway. Thank you, Tariq. Everyone look at Tariq. He is an example to you all. He chose. He wrote it down, not *neatly* exactly, but clear enough to read. And now he's dropped his voting slip in my tub. Thank you, Tariq. *Thank* you. And thank you, Henry. No need to *flick* it in. Thank you, Russ. Thank you. Thank you, Martin, and I hope you'll be very happy wi –'

Mr Cartright broke off. For it was clear the new boy wasn't even listening. As Mr Cartright's shadow fell across his desk, he'd simply pulled the forefinger of his right hand out of that ear for a moment, picked up his neatly written vote, and dropped it in the plastic tub. At no point had he so much as glanced up from his book.

Mr Cartright was mystified. Gently, he prised Martin Simon's fingers out of his ears, and asked him:

'What are you doing?'

Now the boy was equally confused.

'Reading, sir.'

'Reading? Reading what?'

'Baudelaire.'

Mr Cartright's eyes widened.

'*Baudelaire*?'

He glanced round the room, hoping for one mad moment that none of his other pupils had heard the exchange. Fat chance of that. They were all sitting, ears on stalks.

'In French or English?' Mr Cartright asked, thinking to diffuse the tension with a joke.

Young Martin Simon flushed.

Mr Cartright swivelled the book round on the desk.

'French!'

'Sorry,' said Martin Simon automatically. Mr Cartright sighed.

'So am I, lad. So am I.'

There was a pause. Then Mr Cartright said:

'Well? What are you waiting for? Pack your book bag. Off you go.'

Martin Simon looked up in astonishment.

'Go *where*, sir?'

'Anywhere. I should think a lad like you could take your pick. You could try Mr King's class. Or Mr

Henderson's. I bet either of them would be happy to have you.'

'But *why*?'

Mr Cartright settled his huge rear end companionably on Martin Simon's desk. For an intelligent lad, he thought, he wasn't acting too bright.

'Look at it this way,' he told him. 'You can't stay here. For one thing, you can read. You'll be right out of place here from that alone. Then there's the other problem. You read French.'

He waved a hand airily round the room, to draw in the others who were sitting there staring.

'I expect there'll be quite a lot of language in this classroom,' he explained. 'I, for one, have a temper. Then there's the colourful patois of our local housing scheme to be contended with. And Tariq here, I'm told, swears in three separate sub-continental dialects. But no one speaks French.'

He shifted on the desk.

'No,' he said. 'I'm afraid you'll have to go.'

A thought struck him.

'With all those science exams you passed, you could even try Dr Feltham. He might have you.'

At last Martin Simon seemed to grasp the point. Rising to his feet, he started shovelling the few possessions he'd unpacked back into his book bag.

Mr Cartright caught the rather regretful expression on the boy's face.

'I'm sorry about it too, lad,' he said. 'But, believe me, it's for the best. You wouldn't fit in here. There's been some mistake.'

Martin Simon nodded.

'Ask at the office,' Mr Cartright advised, walking him to the door. 'Tell them they've got it all wrong, and you can't come back here. I won't have you. You don't belong.'

He saw him off on the long trek down the green corridor.

'Goodbye, lad,' he called out wistfully after him. 'Good luck!'

He swung the door closed and turned to face the rest with iron determination.

'Right!' he said. 'Put that scarf away, Sajid. Are you eating, Luis Pereira? Spit it out in the bin. Look how much time we've wasted. I warn you, I'm getting this finished before the bell rings.'

With any other class, he might have managed it. But what with two of the tellers he chose not being all that good at counting, and the constant delays as people criticized each way of tallying ('You can't count Rick's vote, sir! He's never here!'), there wasn't time to do it properly. Even before the third recount was complete, Robin Foster and Wayne Driscoll were eyeing him with their imaginary stop-watches raised, and lips pursed round their nonexistent whistles.

It was almost Time …

Mr Cartright slid his vast bulk off the desk on to his feet. Not for nothing was he called Old Carthorse behind his back.

'Hush up!' he bellowed, cutting directly through all the layers of noise at once. 'That's it! I've had enough! The bell's about to ring, and we're wrapping this up one way or another. I warn you, 4C, the very next boy responsible for any noise in this room – *any noise at all* – will have to dip his hand in this tub and take out a voting slip, and whatever it says on that goes.'

The silence was instant and total. High fliers they might not be, but every one of them was bright enough not to fancy the idea of being blamed by all the rest for three solid weeks of work on some project cruelly designed by Dr Feltham to bring out the latent interest of things like sewing or cooking or housekeeping.

It seemed no one dared breathe. Mr Cartright could even hear the warble of a songbird outside on the guttering.

Then, without warning, the spell broke.

The other side of the classroom door suddenly suffered the most tremendous thud. The door knob rattled and the panels shook.

In walked a clumsy young giant.

A roar of approval greeted the newcomer's entrance.

'Hi, nit-face!'

'Last one in class gets maimed!'

'Sime! Saved a place for you!'

'Found us at last, have you, you great fishcake!'

'Get a *brain*, Simon Martin!'

Simon Martin ... Martin Simon ... Of course.

Mr Cartright heaved himself back into his usual

position on the desk. So there was the explanation. Simple enough. Mere clerical error.

Martin Simon … Simon Martin …

He let the flurry of excitement ride for a few moments longer.

'Where've you *been*, Sime?'

'Got stuck, din't I?' declared the newcomer proudly. 'In Dr Feltham's class.'

'Dr Feltham's!'

Another roar of laughter, and even Mr Cartright had to smile, trying to picture this huge, strapping and unthinking lad marooned amongst Dr Feltham's boffins.

'*Tole* him I din't *blong*. But would he listen? Not him. Not till that other ear'ole finally came along and rescued me. And even then –'

To cut off what was clearly all set to develop into a prolonged riff of resentment, Mr Cartright held the plastic tub of votes out towards his brand new pupil.

'Pick one,' he said.

Simon Martin's look of deep disgruntlement turned into one of even deeper suspicion.

'Wossit for?'

'Just pick one.' Mr Cartright sharpened the tone to an order. 'Now.'

Simon Martin reached in and picked the one that happened to be written most neatly.

'What does it say?'

The lad stared at it for a few moments. His massive

caterpillar eyebrows crumpled in confusion as he struggled with Martin Simon's perfect handwriting. Then:

'Chile ... chile ... chile dev-lop-ment,' he read aloud stumblingly.

'Development.'

Mr Cartright managed to slide in the correction a split second before the explosion.

'That's *babies*, isn't it?'

'We're not doing *babies*, sir!'

'That *is* girls' stuff. It is!'

'I shan't be coming in at all now! Not till it's all over, anyhow.'

'I'm blaming you, Sime!'

'You can't call it *science*. It's just a great big *cheat*!'

'Pick again, Sime!'

Hastily, Mr Cartright upended the tub over the waste bin. The remaining votes floated down to join whatever it was Luis Pereira had spat in earlier.

Mr Cartright flicked through the pages of Dr Feltham's vast Science Fair memorandum. Oh, what a ghastly way to start the term! Why couldn't the man arrange things the way every other school did, and leave the great tribute to the wonders of science until the last couple of weeks before the holidays, when classes like 4C could be left peaceably slacking? That was the trouble with enthusiasts, of course. They never allowed for other people's weaknesses.

Finding the right page at last, Mr Cartright raised his

voice like someone announcing the winner of an Oscar, and declared solemnly:

'And the experiment Dr Feltham has chosen for this topic is –'

He glanced round. He hadn't even said it yet, and already a sea of disgusted faces was staring back at him.

'Flour babies!'

Now scorn was supplanted by confusion.

'Sir?'

'Is that *flour* babies or *flower* babies?'

'They both sound weird to me.'

'What *are* they?'

'Whatever they are, they don't sound much like proper *Science.*'

Secretly, that was what Mr Cartright thought. He glanced at the list again. Could it be a mistake? Another clerical error?

No. There it was, clear as paint.

Flour babies.

Right.

Mr Cartright slapped Dr Feltham's memorandum down on the desk. Whatever they were, there was no time to read about them now. Already, Wayne Driscoll's cheeks were puffed to bursting, and he was waving his imaginary stopwatch about wildly.

And, sure enough, the bell rang.

Just one more short ritual to get through, and the lesson would be over. Who would be first today?

Bill Simmons.

'Excuse me, Bill Simmons. I don't remember anyone telling you this lesson was over. Back in your seat, please.'

'But, sir! Sir! The bell's rung.'

'That bell's for me, Bill. It is not for you.'

His heart wasn't in it, though. No, not today. In fact, to get rid of them just that little bit sooner, he even stooped to pretending he hadn't seen Russ Mould's bottom hovering an insolent ten inches clear of the chair, ready to make the big getaway.

'All right, 4C. Off you go.'

They hurled themselves at the door in a disorderly rabble, leaving him wondering.

Flour babies … What on earth?

Notes for Chapter 2

Having seen 4C from Mr Cartright's viewpoint in Chapter 1, the writer now introduces us to the main character in the novel, Simon Martin. We see school and the teachers in it, from a very different viewpoint: Simon's own. The things he finds interesting and frustrating are very different from those his teacher does.

What do you think?
Think about what Simon finds difficult at school and what he enjoys. Are these experiences at school educating him for adult life or not?

Questions
1. Look at the conversation between Dr Feltham and Mr Cartright. Consider the clues in their language that show the differences between the two men. You could represent this in two columns, using evidence from the text to support your answers.
2. Look at the description of Simon's pleasure on hearing about the exploding flour, beginning 'The vision was so beguiling …' (page 27). What exactly does it mean?
3. Look through Mr Cartright's conversation with 4C about their choice of project. What sly techniques does he use to try to get his own way?
4. Thinking carefully about the way Anne Fine began the novel. What do you think about the last line of this chapter? What technique is she using to make us read on?

Further activity
At the beginning of the chapter Simon is feeling bored. Look at the metaphors (comparisons that omit the words 'like' or 'as') below that Simon might have written. Write out some of your own that sum up boredom for you. You might like to turn these into a poem.

Boredom is…
Boredom is sitting outside the staff room having been sent out of assembly
Boredom is whistling to pass the time and then being told off for it
Boredom is spending miserable hours scraping my massive knees under the dolly desks at school … Boredom is …

24

Chapter 2

Simon Martin sprawled over the three chairs outside the staffroom door. He'd been sent there for being a nuisance in Assembly. He'd only arrived four minutes earlier, and already he was bored halfway out of his skull. He'd tried whistling (and been told off for it by Miss Arnott on her way in). He'd tried tapping tunes with his feet (and been told off for it by Mr Henderson on his way out). He'd even tried seeing how many different clicking noises he could make with his tongue (and been told off for it by Mr Spencer as he walked past).

They'd left him no choice, really.

They couldn't expect him to sit there all day doing nothing.

When the next teacher came out, he'd give it a go.

The next teacher to come out was Mr Dupasque. As the door swung behind him, Simon Martin surreptitiously shifted one of his quite enormous feet a couple of inches backwards and used his heel to stop the door from closing properly.

It was their own fault. If they didn't want someone who had already been picked on in Assembly for no reason at all getting so bored he ended up listening to what they were saying, they should have left him alone while he was peacefully whistling and tapping and clicking.

Simon settled in for a good eavesdrop. In fact, if he turned his head to the right as if he were gazing down the corridor, he could even see a thin slice of staffroom out of the corner of his eye. Across it, Old Carthorse was reeling, making one of his giant great fusses.

'I don't believe this,' Mr Cartright was bellowing. 'I cannot believe my *ears.* Are you seriously trying to tell me that these child development project things of yours are literally six pounds of plain white flour sewn into a sacking bag? And you intend to give one of these things to each of the maniacs in my class?'

'Not give, Eric. Lend.'

'Give. Lend.' Simon caught a brief glimpse of a slice of Mr Cartright's arms, thrown up in a gesture of despair. 'With that pack of sociopaths, what difference does it make? No one in 4C could take care of a *stone* without cracking it. You can't expect six-pound bags of flour to survive!'

Through the gap, Simon saw a strip of Dr Feltham's anxious face.

'Not six pounds, Eric. Three kilos. Now do try to set an example. Think in grammes.'

'I'll think how I damn well want, thank you,' Simon overheard Mr Cartright growl. 'And, frankly, I think you must be off your trolley. There are nineteen boys in 4C this term, you know. Nineteen times six is one hundred and twenty three!'

'One hundred and fourteen,' Dr Feltham couldn't help correcting.

'*What?*'

Dr Feltham mistook Mr Cartright's mixture of

impatience and outrage for a sincere quest for mathematical enlightenment.

'I think you must have multiplied the nine by seven by mistake,' he said. 'It's the only rational explanation for that particular error.'

What with all this fancy talk of numbers, Simon's attention was flagging. He was about to slide his foot forward and let the door close again, when another slice of Mr Cartright reeled into view, and he heard his class teacher howl.

'Hundred and this! Hundred and that! What does it matter? It's still over a hundred pounds of sifted white flour exploding in my classroom!'

Outside in the corridor, a look of sheer rapture spread over young Simon Martin's face. Could he be hearing right? One hundred pounds of sifted white flour? Exploding? In the classroom? Oh, bliss and joy! Worth coming back to school. Worth all the miserable hours spent scraping his massive knees under the dolly desks, being moaned at by teachers, and shrivelling with boredom.

One hundred pounds of sifted white flour.
BANG!!!!!

Oh, he could see it now. Drifts of it! Mountains of it! Clouds of it! The room would be knee-deep in flour. It would rain flour. Flour would puff out of the windows, track from the door.

The vision was so beguiling, so white and perfect, so absolutely beautiful, that Simon's ears were temporarily blocked by the ballooning magic force of his imagination, and he completely missed Dr Feltham's attempt to explain the experiment to his colleague.

'You've got it all *wrong*, Eric. It's the custard tins that explode, not the flour babies. The flour babies are a simple experiment in parent and child relationships. Each boy takes full responsibility for his flour baby for the whole three weeks, keeping a diary to chart his problems and attitudes. It's quite interesting what comes out. It's fascinating what they learn, about themselves and about parenthood. It's a very worthwhile experiment. You wait and see.'

Simon caught only the last words, 'Wait and see'. But he was seeing it already! *BANG!!!!* And then a floury mushroom cloud obliterating the hated prison of the classroom. He rose in spirit with its snow-white glory, and only floated down in time to overhear the last of Mr Cartright's desperate attempts to turn down this astonishing and unparalleled blessing.

'Why can't they do something in Mr Higham's workshops?'

A new voice now, raised in anguish.

'Eric! My workshops are buzzing! It's the Science Fair! Why, there's the slopes to set up for the slope friction experiment. And the skeleton house to build for 4F's electronic burglar alarm system. The base for Harrison's thermistor-powered fan hasn't even been begun yet. Nor has the frame for the Hughes twins' electric power station. Even the maggot farm needs a few repairs, or we'll have maggots all over.'

Simon saw a flash of Mr Higham in the gap, spreading his hands.

'I'm sorry, Eric. It's more than my job's worth to let your crowd into the workshops at the moment. Last time I frisked Rick Tullis on the way out, he had four of my screwdrivers stuck down his underpants. Four! And that Sajid Mahmoud of yours only has to *look* at a wood plane for its blade to slip out of true. I'm sorry, Eric. But no.'

If Simon hadn't been so outraged with Mr Cartright for trying to spurn this gift sent from the gods, he might have felt pity at the broken tone of his voice now.

'I won't forget this,' Mr Cartright was saying. 'Next time any of you are in a fix, I shall remember this!'

Prudently, Simon drew his heel back as the voice neared the doorway.

'One hundred and twenty four pounds of white flour! In my classroom! With that bunch! And not one of you came to my rescue. Not one. I shan't forget this. No. I shan't forget.'

Simon's foot moved sharply away from the door, just as Mr Cartright wrenched it open.

'What are you doing here?'

'You *tole* me to come here, sir.'

'Well, now I'm telling you different. Go away. Go back to the classroom at once.'

'Yes, sir.'

On principle, Simon stooped, quite unnecessarily, to

untie his shoelace and tie it again, in his own time. He wasn't sorry he took the trouble, either, because although the small gesture of defiance earned him a quite alarming glare from Mr Cartright, it also kept them both standing there long enough to hear, unmistakably clearly, from inside:

'He's got it wrong again, you know. This time he must have multiplied the one by a seven. It's odd the way his mind works.'

Satisfied that honours were now even, Simon shambled off. And Mr Cartright shambled after him. He let the boy draw ahead down the long corridor, to give himself time to think. What was the best thing to do? True, he'd made a firm announcement that the very next boy to make any noise at all would have to choose the topic. And Simon had picked the flour babies. But, fair's fair, the lad's neanderthal door-wrenching habits were purely accidental. He hadn't been trying it on. He just naturally opened doors like a gorilla.

No need to hold firm unnecessarily.

They could just choose again.

Cheered, Mr Cartright speeded up. Working things out, he'd fallen quite a way behind. Far enough behind, in fact, to miss Simon Martin's breathless announcement to the waiting class as he burst through the door first.

'Them flour babies! They're dead brilliant! Better than soap, and maggots, and everything! Best science I've ever *heard*!'

Rolling in twenty seconds later, Mr Cartright doused

down the noise without even bothering to tune in to its content. He heaved his rump up on the teacher's desk, and began in a conciliatory fashion.

'Well now, 4C, I'm a reasonable man, and it seems to me on reflection that there's no reason why you should all suffer from the noise Simon Martin makes opening a door. One day, when we have a little more time, we'll explain to him about the principles and use of the door handle. But right now I think we can let bygones be bygones, and go back to discussing the options for the Science Fair.'

Simon sucked air in sharply between his teeth. He didn't, on the whole, pay much attention to teachers. But he did recognize their cunning in all its common forms.

'Old Smoothy-chops!' he muttered bitterly to his neighbour at the next desk, Robin Foster. 'He's just trying to wriggle out of the flour babies because they're the *best*.'

Out of sheer habit, Robin passed this intelligence on. So did his neighbour. So did his. The whisper swept round the room so fast that by the time Mr Cartright beamed brightly and asked,

'Now, who'd prefer textiles?'
they were ranked up and ready with their own form of sabotage.

'Sewing and stuff! Great! You watch out, Foster! I owe you a good stabbing with the unpicker, back from first year.'

'Bet I can stick fifty pins in my face, and keep them there the whole lesson!'

'Bet Tariq can make the sewing machine go so fast it *busts.*'

'Can I make a Nazi flag, please, sir?'

'If it's textiles, can we do *stains*?'

'Oh, yes, sir! Yes! I can think of some great stains which wouldn't wash out. *Never.*'

Inwardly, Mr Cartright shuddered.

'Tell you what,' he said brightly. 'Let's not bother with textiles. Let's just make it consumer studies instead.'

But they were already lying in wait for him on this one.

'Yeh! Yeh!'

'Done consumer studies before. It was dead good. Once we had to count how many baked beans there were in eight different sorts of cans. Our team would have won, sir, except for Wayne pigging so many.'

'We would have won the value-for-money-in-sweeties test, too, sir. But Tariq kept spitting them at Phil instead of sucking them properly.'

None of this sort of soft stuff was likely to daunt Mr Cartright, Simon could tell. If they were to succeed in their unspoken purpose of making sure everything except flour babies was right out of favour, someone had to roll out the big guns.

'You're let off down the shops in consumer studies,' he threatened Mr Cartright darkly.

And, promptly, the others came up trumps.

'Yeh! Only four of our lot came back once. Poor Mr Harris took a major fit.'

'And Russ nearly got run over. That was a laugh.'

'This man jumped out of his car, and as soon as he'd checked Russ was all right, he bashed him.'

'Just for making a dent in his bumper, sir. And it wasn't my fault. Luis pushed me.'

'Luis was chasing a girl.'

Luis gazed round the room proudly.

'Met Moira, though, didn't I?'

At the mere mention of Moira's name, there were animal roars of approval. Mr Cartright turned his back on the lot of them. He didn't want to have to see the rush of arcane and dubious gestures he knew from experience greeted any female name. In any case, he found the whole idea of sending them trailing round the shops utterly dispiriting. Why had schools been invented, for heaven's sake? Surely to fill young people's minds with loftier things than knowing how best to shop for floorcloths.

No, he'd have nothing to do with this new-fangled philistinism.

He picked up the board rubber, and with two long, firm strokes, wiped textiles and consumer studies off the board.

'How about domestic economy?' he suggested.

Cries of contempt rang round.

'Wendy Houses!'

'Let's pretend!'

'Oh, golly me! You mustn't use that cloth to wipe the plates. You've just used it down the lavatory!'

'Bring in your washing when it rains, or, guess what! It might get wet!'

'You must be making all this up,' Mr Cartright accused them sternly. But for the life of him, he couldn't think what else domestic economy might be about, except stuff that any half-wit could work out for himself in a fortnight.

He rubbed domestic economy off the board.

'You realize,' he said, 'That only leaves babies and food.'

He was convinced that this would settle it. After all, most of the boys in front of him spent half the day industriously filling their faces. You could barely get through a lesson without having to order one or another of them to swallow this, or spit out that, or wrap up the other and put it away until break time. He should be home and dry on food.

But, no.

'We've done nutrition before, sir. It didn't have anything to do with food.'

'It's all writing.'

'Choosing recipes.'

Wayne Driscoll did one of his laborious brain searches, and rather triumphantly came up with a phrase unwittingly committed to memory in first year.

'Well-balanced meals, sir!'

'What two old codgers with wobbly teeth might have for breakfast.'

'It's dead boring.'

'No cooking.'

'Just looking at charts and stuff.'

Mr Cartright was mystified. What was the point of the

taxpayer lashing out on giant gleaming kitchens in schools all over the country if the pupils didn't even use them?

'You must have cooked sometimes,' he insisted.

The scowl Sajid Mahmoud turned on him would have frightened stone.

'The only time I got to cook,' he said, 'I got a giant great row for scraping it in the bin after it had been marked.'

'I should think so!' said Mr Cartright. 'What a waste!'

'I couldn't eat it though, could I? It was meat stew, and I don't eat meat.'

'You should have chosen to prepare something different.'

Sajid burned with refreshed outrage at the ancient injustice.

'Why? Nobody said a thing about *eating* it! Nobody even so much as *mentioned* eating it. They went on and on about it being all well-balanced, like Wayne says, and having vitamins and such. But nobody ever said a thing about liking it or eating it.'

He relapsed into furious muttering.

'And the Old Meanie changed my B to an F. *And* made me rinse out the bin ...'

'What about the rest of you?' interrupted Mr Cartright. And with what he thought was real cunning, he offered Simon a chance to shed all the responsibility for having accidentally picked the wrong option in the first place. 'How about you, Simon? You'd prefer cooking, wouldn't you?'

Simon gave him a low-grade glower.

'No, I wouldn't.'

'Really?' Mr Cartright persisted. 'Surely a growing lad like you enjoys the odd plate of extra fodder.'

But Simon had no intention of letting himself be won over. Nor of letting any of the rest of the class be seduced without remembering the grim facts of yester-year.

'We could have *starved*,' he said. 'We could have keeled over and *died* before we got round to actual cooking. First we spent weeks and weeks learning how to change ounces into grammes, and then we spent weeks and weeks learning how to change them back again, and then we were nagged about eating fibroids –'

'Fibres, surely.'

'Whatever.' Simon shrugged off the correction. 'But we only got to go in the kitchen twice the whole term.'

He couldn't resist adding bitterly:

'And, one of those times, half of us got sent out practically right at the start, just for standing quietly in a line.'

Mr Cartright gave him a look.

'Standing quietly in line? Like in Assembly this morning when I sent you out?'

'Quieter than that,' Simon responded virtuously.

'That's right, sir,' Robin Foster backed Simon up. 'We were all queuing.'

'Queuing to use the food processor.'

'Needed to slice our tomatoes, didn't we?'

And, suddenly, Mr Cartright could see it. A vision, as if

it were in front of him, as if it were this morning. A whole class of them, mucking about in a line, pushing and shoving and jostling and cat-calling one another. Half of them holding their tomatoes so carelessly that watery red drips wept on the gleaming floor tiles. The rest spurting slimy yellow tomato pips as far as possible up the walls, or into one another's faces.

'Queuing,' he said. 'Just queuing quietly?'

'That's right,' all the ones who had been there assured him.

Mr Cartright had put up a good fight. But he was cracking now. Simon couldn't help grinning with pleasure and relief as, watching his form teacher intently, he spotted the very moment at which nutrition, as an option, lost its appeal. All Mr Cartright could see now, in his mind's eye, was a line of boys queuing for the food processor. Each one prepared to waste almost a whole lesson standing in line, simply in order to get a turn on that magical whirring and whining machine. Each boy frittering away half an hour of his short life waiting to drop one poor battered lone tomato into the fat round bowel of that precision appliance with all its switches, blades and speeds. Each boy slowly and impatiently inching forward, ignoring utterly the simple, humble kitchen knife with which, within seconds – no fuss, no mess – he could have chopped or sliced or diced his tomato.

Life was too short for nutrition.

Let it be flour babies. Let chaos reign.

Notes for Chapter 3

During this chapter Simon begins to develop an understanding of himself and the significant responsibility of parenthood. While his mother and his friends think he is behaving strangely, the role of looking after his flour baby seems to be making him consider himself, his own childhood and the things his mother has said to him in the past. It also makes him think about his own father and try to find out more about him.

What do you think?
Study the section from the beginning of the chapter to 'He had a question for his mother now, though' (page 45). Anne Fine moves from the 'now' of the story back in time to other events. Can you pinpoint the two places where she does this?

Questions
Look carefully for evidence in the text to answer the following questions.
1. What is Mr Cartright's opinion of teachers like Dr Feltham?
2. Robin is worried about Simon's behaviour: 'he glanced at Simon, trying to work out if he had been joking. Finally, from the quiver of possible responses, he chose the sharpest arrow: ridicule' (page 42). Why is Robin's store of responses described as a quiver and ridicule described as an arrow? Can you explain the image that is being used?
3. What does this chapter show about Mrs Martin's character and the kind of mother she is?

Further activity
Imagine you are a member of 4C frustrated with the flour babies' rules given out in class. For English homework you have been told to pick a piece of text, underline the verbs and then change some of the verbs to see if you can change the meaning of the sentence. See if you can do this for the flour babies' rules. You may like to add illustrations. An example is completed for you below:

4. You must *steal* a Baby Book, and *scribble* in it daily. Each entry should be no shorter than three full sentences, and no longer than five pages.

Chapter 3

Simon sat across the kitchen table from his flour baby and gave her a poke.

The flour baby fell over.

'Ha!' Simon scoffed. 'Can't even sit up yet!'

He set the flour baby up again, and gave her another poke.

Again, she fell over.

'Not very good at standing up for yourself, are you?' Simon taunted, setting her up again.

The flour baby fell over backwards this time, off the table into the dog basket.

'Blast!'

'You mustn't swear in front of it,' Simon's mother said. 'You'll set it a terrible example.'

Simon reached down to scoop the flour baby off Macpherson's cushion, and picked the dog's hairs off her frock.

'Not *it*,' he reproved his mum in turn. '*Her.*' She was definitely a her. Definitely. Some of the flour babies Mr Cartright had handed out that morning could have been one or the other. It wasn't clear. But not the one that landed in Simon's lap.

'Catch, Dozy! Aren't you supposed to be one of the school's sporting heroes? Wake up!'

She was *sweet*. She was dressed in a frilly pink bonnet and a pink nylon frock, and carefully painted on her sacking were luscious sexy round eyes fringed with fluttering lashes.

Robin Foster, beside him, was jealous instantly.

'How come you get one with eyes? Mine's just plain sacking. Do you want to swap?'

Simon tightened his grip round his flour baby.

'No. She's mine. You paint eyes on your own if you want them.'

'And yours has clothes!' He turned to yell at Mr Cartright, who was just coming to the end of tossing bags of flour round the room. 'Sir! Sir! Sime's dolly has got a frock and a bonnet and eyes and everything. And mine's got nothing. It's not fair.'

'If every parent who had a baby who was a bit lacking sent it back,' Mr Cartright said. 'This classroom would be practically empty. Sit down and be quiet.'

He heaved himself up on the desk, and started reading the rules of the experiment.

FLOUR BABIES

1. The flour babies must be kept clean and dry at all times. All fraying, staining and leakage of stuffing will be taken very seriously indeed.
2. Flour babies will be put on the official scales twice a week to check for any weight loss that might indicate casual neglect or maltreatment, or any weight gain that might indicate tampering or damp.
3. No flour baby may be left unattended at any time, night or day. If you *must* be out of sight of your flour baby, even for a short time, a responsible babysitter must be arranged.
4. You must keep a Baby Book, and write in it daily. Each entry should be no shorter than three full sentences, and no longer than five pages.

5. Certain persons (who shall not be named until the experiment is over) shall make it their business to check on the welfare of the flour babies and the keeping of the above rules. These people may be parents, other pupils, or members of staff or the public.

He looked up.

'That's it.'

He'd never seen a class reduced to silence before. An interesting sight. You had to hand it to Dr Feltham and these boffin types. They had weird powers. Some of them might fumble in and out of the staffroom, letting their woollies unravel behind them, and visibly having to trawl through their memory banks each time someone asked them if they took sugar in their tea. But they could work wonders. They could wreak miracles. With their mysterious arts, they could do the unimaginable. They could blow the whole planet to smithereens. They could silence 4C.

'Well?' he asked, somewhat unnerved. 'Any questions?'

Simon picked up his flour baby and lifted her frock. No knickers, unless you counted sacking bag. Already she had black smudges on her bum where he'd sat her on the pen runnel of the double desk along which Robin Foster's rubber dropping collection had recently overflowed.

'Now look at that,' he complained to Robin. 'She's already dirty, and it's your fault, Foster.

'You're going to have to keep this desk a whole lot cleaner in future.'

Robin stared down at the little heaps of filthy rubbing-out scurf, assiduously kept so he and Simon would always have raw material for flicking pellets. Then he glanced at Simon, trying to work out if he had been joking. Finally, from the quiver of possible responses, he chose the sharpest arrow: ridicule.

'Sir! Sir!' he'd yelled, his fist punching the air as he called for the whole room's attention. 'You've got to move me, sir. I can't stay here. It's not safe. Sime Martin's turning into my mother!'

They kept the joke up for the rest of the day. By the time the last bell rang, Simon was absolutely sick of having to prop his flour baby carefully on top of his book bag, then go after whoever it was who'd last called him Old Mrs Martin, or Mother Sime, and bash their head hard against the wall. By the time he shambled out of the back gate at half past three, his knuckles were burning and his wrist badly grazed. He only stopped himself wiping the blood off on the flour baby's frock because, through some miracle, he heard the echo of his mother's voice ring out of nowhere in his ears: 'Oh, no, Simon! Not blood! It's the *worst!*' He wiped his hand clean down his shirt instead.

And now here was his mother in the flesh, spooning out more free advice.

'You ought to put it in a plastic bag. Keep it clean.'

'Is that what you did with me?'

His mother laughed as she dumped his supper down in front of him. Egg and beans.

'I wish I'd had the sense.'

She was joking, he supposed. But still, it was a thought.

42

Having him must have made all the difference. He'd come along, a whole other person to be taken into account. Real, too. Not just something like a flour baby that could be shoved in a plastic bag to be kept clean, without fetching up on some murder charge. When had she realized how much trouble he was going to be? Some pennies took time to drop. He himself could still remember the day, not that long ago, when he'd first realized he was a person.

He'd been having it out with a turkey. Behind the caravan park where Simon and his mother went on holiday there was a farm, and one of the larger turkeys had pushed its bad-tempered, gobbling way through the fence and was giving Simon the eye – well, first one eye then the other – and stopping him getting to the lavatories.

Simon got his own back the simplest way he could.

'Christmas!' he jeered. 'Din-dins!'

The turkey gobbled off. But Simon had to sit on the lavatory steps for a moment. He'd suddenly realized that by Christmas Day the turkey would really be dead on a plate, but (barring the sort of daft accidents his mother was always going on about), he, Simon, would still be alive.

And somehow that set him off thinking. He pulled the flesh on the back of his hand up into a miniature tent, and then let go. The skin sprang back instantly, keeping him in shape. His shape. It struck Simon for the first time in his life that he was totally unique. In the whole history of the universe, there had never been one of him before. There would never be another.

'Not a very nice place to sit.'

Someone was stepping over him to get to the urinals. But Simon, off on another tack, scarcely heard. Once, only a few years ago, Simon *wasn't* – didn't exist at all. And one day, like that turkey, he wouldn't exist again. Ever.

'Can't you find somewhere a bit more *salubrious* to sit?'

The same fellow again, on his way out. Simon paid no attention, his mind on other things. Hadn't he just discovered himself – him – the one and only Sime Martin, alive, and (unlike the turkey) knowing it?

From that day on, Simon had looked at himself with a whole new respect, a far greater interest. The other holiday-makers became almost accustomed to seeing the lad from the end plot contorting himself into odd shapes, not like the family near the showerhuts who did yoga, but simply in order to gaze at parts of his body he'd never really looked at properly before: heels, elbows, belly button, inner thighs.

'God knows which bits of himself he stares at in private!'

'Do you suppose the poor boy's *mental*?'

'It's his mother I feel sorry for really.'

'Do stop that, Simon! People will think you've got *lice*.'

Neither the neighbours' whispered comments nor his mother's sharp orders grazed Simon's consciousness. He was busy. Busy probing his huge, lank body with a curiosity, a real wonder, he'd never felt before. All that went through his brain was 'This is *me*'. But there was more to it than that, much more, though he could never have explained it, and, in the time between, no one had ever asked him.

He had a question for his mother now, though. Picking the last of Macpherson's wiry hairs off the flour baby, he asked:

'What was I like?'

His mother sucked a stray bean off her fingertip.

'When?'

'When I was a baby.'

Simon's mother narrowed her eyes at him across the table. Give a boy a dolly, she thought, sighing inwardly, and he goes all broody within minutes. What hope is there for girls?

But it was a fair question, and he hadn't asked it for a good few years. Her son deserved an honest answer.

'You were *sweet*,' she said. 'Good as gold, and chubby as a bun, and you had bright button eyes. You were so lovely that perfect strangers kept stopping the pram in the street to coo at you and tell me how lucky I was to have you. Everybody wanted to blow raspberries on your tummy. No doubt about it, you were the most beautiful baby in the world.'

He knew she wouldn't want him to spoil things by saying it, but he couldn't help himself.

'So why did my dad push off so quickly?'

His mother tried her usual tack of making a joke of the whole business.

'Be fair, Simon. He did hang around for six whole weeks!'

But she could tell from the look on his face that the answer wasn't working the way it usually did. So she tried throwing in her Old Crone imitation.

'And there be those who say he could see into the future ...'

But still Simon wouldn't smile.

Mrs Martin gave up, and took another mouthful of her supper, watching him carefully to try and work out exactly how upset he was.

Simon propped the flour baby up in front of him, and stared at her beautiful round eyes. He felt sour all over suddenly. Suppose his dad *was* able to see the future. Did that make up for Simon not being able to see the past? Anyone who'd ever met their real dad could put it together somehow. Take off some middle-aged spread. Wipe out a few wrinkles. Add a bit of hair. But if you'd never so much as *seen* the man –

'Why aren't there any photographs? I know you didn't have a proper wedding or anything, but why aren't there any other photos?'

'Simon! There are photos! There are *lots*.'

'But not with him. There's hardly a single one of him.'

'That's because he was usually the one holding the camera.'

'You could have taken at least one good photo of him.'

She jammed her tea spoon back in the sugar bowl so hard that sugar flew out and sprayed all over.

'And how was I supposed to know he was going to walk out on me? Women don't always get a week's notice, you know!'

Simon stuck out his tongue, and after a small, insolent pause, began licking the grains of spilled sugar from his wrists. Then he turned his attention to the flour baby.

'Don't lick her, Simon!' And then, instead of adding, 'She's been in the dog basket', his mother warned him: 'You might give her germs.'

It wasn't a very good joke. But the fact that she'd bothered to try and make one at all made Simon feel better. He realized that, for all she made light of it whenever the business of his father came up, she did understand he had reasons of his own to feel sensitive about the matter. Shovelling the last forkful of beans into his mouth, he asked indistinctly:

'When did you first realize I was a real person?'

He didn't know what answer he was expecting. Maybe 'When you were eight', (when he'd refused to go to Hyacinth Spicer's party). Even 'As young as four' (when he'd apparently thrown such a tantrum in a shoe shop that the manager herself had stepped over and slapped him).

But what she said really astonished him.

'Oh, weeks before you were born! I think we must have been in different time zones. If I was up and about, you were so restful you might not have been there at all. But the moment I lay my head on a pillow, you woke up and set about kicking me.'

'Football practice, see?' he said proudly.

And that reminded him. He glanced at the clock. First session of the term. Mustn't be late.

'Time to go.'

His mother lifted her knife and fork, and slid his plate on to hers.

'Don't let the little lady get muddy,' she warned, nodding at the flour baby. 'Make sure you put her somewhere safe.'

Simon was horrified.

'I can't take it to football!'

'Not *it*, Simon. *Her.*'

Irritably, he brushed off the tease.

'How can I take her to *football*?'

'You have to take her, Simon. It's in those rules you brought home.'

Simon cast about desperately for some reason not to take her.

'I can't! It's not just people from our class, you know. There's only me and Wayne from our class on the team. Everyone else will see. They'll fall about laughing. We'll get crucified!'

'Just keep her out of sight.'

'Mu-*um*!' Had the woman never been in a locker room? Didn't she know your sports bag was not your own? You would be lucky if one time in the whole season you got away without having some joker root through your kit to tug out your underpants and make a great drama of sniffing them and whirling them about, or even just borrowing your deodorant or nicking your bus fare.

He'd give a flour baby doll a life expectancy of minutes in a locker room.

Less.

'You'll have to look after it, Mum.'

'Me?'

'Just while I'm gone.'

She put on her Forget-it-Simon look.

'Forget it, Simon. I'm out myself until nine. If you think I'm taking your homework with me –'

Simon made his mind up.

'She can just stay here. She'll be all right. It's perfectly safe. I'll shut Macpherson in the living room, so he won't chew her or anything. She'll be fine.'

There was a glint in Simon's mother's eye. Amusement? Interest? Mischief? He couldn't tell.

'And what about Rule 5?'

Rule 5? The snoopers! Simon snatched the list of rules towards him and struggled through Rule 5 again.

Certain persons (who shall not be named until the experiment is over) shall make it their business to check on the welfare of the flour babies and the keeping of the above rules. These people may be parents, other pupils, or members of staff or the public.

Members of staff! Old Carthorse must know about the football. What had he said this morning when he tossed the flour baby over? 'Aren't you supposed to be one of the school's sporting heroes?' Maybe he'd make it his

49

business to sneak along and rummage through the changing rooms, looking for his and Wayne's babies.

And 'other pupils'. Maybe he'd ordered someone else to check up on both of them. Maybe that Jimmy Holdcroft had been signed on secretly as a nark. He was an oily piece of work. Being a stool pigeon would be right up his street.

And 'members of the public'. Next door was always twitching her curtains. She was a natural spy. She'd love to gang up with the enemy. All in a day's work for Mrs Spicer.

No. When it came down to it, no one was safe. You didn't know if you could trust your own mother ...

His eyes fell on the snooper rule again. 'These people may be parents ...'

Slowly, casually, he turned to look at her. That glint! It was still in her eye!

Oh, surely not. Surely not his own mother. The very idea was ridiculous.

Except –

They'd do *anything*, these parents, if they thought it was good for you, or for your education. In this respect, she had no pride at all. Didn't he know from bitter experience that there were no depths to which she wouldn't sink? Over the years she'd done everything to try and improve his school record. Threats. Bribes. Even punishments. She'd stopped his allowance. She'd grounded him. She'd yelled. She'd begged. Sometimes she'd even cried. (That was the worst.)

Spying on him would be chicken-feed. It would be *nothing* to a mother like her. She'd take it in her stride.

He couldn't trust her. No, he couldn't trust her.

Sighing, Simon lifted his flour baby off the table and wrapped her carefully in his Tottenham Hotspur towel, so just her eyes were peeking out.

'Right,' he said. 'Off we go. Your first football practice. I hope I'm not going to have to remind you how to behave. And I suppose that, on the way, I'm going to have to explain all the rules.'

Mrs Martin moved to the window to watch her son striding down the path, explaining the rules of football to a small flour sack with a bonnet and eyes, wrapped up in a Tottenham Hotspur bath towel. She wasn't the only one paying attention, she noticed. Next door's curtains were twitching. Mrs Spicer was watching too.

And Simon saw. Turning at the gate, he spotted next door's golden brushed-velour curtains shivering in the still air. He broke off his explanation of how an indirect free kick differs from a corner, and, leaning closer to his flour baby, whispered in the pointy bit he took to be her ear:

'You can't trust anyone, you know. No. Not round here.'

Notes for Chapter 4

In Chapter 4 we see Anne Fine developing her novel in terms of ideas, character development and the way the story is built up. The theme of growing up is addressed. Simon's character begins to change and mature. She continues to use flashbacks to tell us more about Simon's past. As we become familiar with Simon's emotions, school life and family situation we start to sympathise with him.

What do you think?
In Chapter 4 we can still see traces of the less well-behaved Simon we met in Chapter 1, as well as the newer, more mature boy. See if you can spot both elements of his personality as you read through.

Questions
1. Look at the section where Simon spends time finding a hiding place for his flour baby. He says the reason is so that he does not get thrown off the project and miss The Glorious Explosion. Do you think this is the real reason? Support your answer with proof from the text.
2. Decide which three of the following words best describe Simon's thoughts about his father. Make sure you can give reasons for your choices: unfair; loving; romantic; unreal; passionate; spiteful; childish; realistic; unhappy; glorious; sarcastic; exuberant; original.
3. What is the name for the 'comma thing' (page 53) Simon mentions, in the word *Athlete's*? Look at the first page of this chapter and locate two different examples of how this punctuation mark is used. Explain them to a partner.

Further activity
Trace the changes in Simon's character in this chapter that show he is starting to act and think like a parent. Set them out in a chart as below:

What he does/thinks	Quotation	What this shows about his character

Chapter 4

Boot … Boot … Boot … Boot …

Mr Fuller's bellow reached Simon across the length of the football pitch.

'Don't *boot* it, lad! *Tickle* it.'

It was Simon's third and last circuit. He was quite fortunate, really. Last year, any member of the team who showed up so late had to do fifty press-ups. Compared with that, dribbling the ball three times round the pitch was a doddle. Old Fuller must be going soft.

Boot … Boot … Boot … Boot …

'Are you going cloth-eared, boy? You're not practising goal kicks! Chase the ball *gently*! Keep it under control. I want to be able to see the elastic holding it to your feet.'

It wasn't his fault he'd been late. He blamed Wayne. If Wayne hadn't dragged him off through the empty classrooms, rooting through desks to find that bottle of Tippex …

Good laugh, though. Pity he wasn't back in the changing rooms with the rest to see Froggie's face when he picked up his tin of foot powder and read what it said on the side now:

Kills Athletes

Brilliant.

It was Wayne's idea to paint out the word *Foot*. But it was Simon who guessed the comma thing in *Athlete's* ought to go too. He wasn't sure. It was just a hunch. But hunches were sometimes right. What about the time he'd been fetched out to stand beside Miss Arnott's desk for mucking about in English? She'd been marking some essay of Gwyn Phillip's called 'My Summer Holiday', and muttering to herself under her breath. Then, raising her voice, she'd asked irritably:

'What is this rubbish you've written, Gwyn? *"The Italians are all retarded and fiendish"*?'

Gwyn Phillips had looked (baffled.) How would he know? He hadn't been on holiday at all. He'd copied the whole thing from Bill Simmons, without thinking. But Simon, peering over Miss Arnott's glorious golden summer holiday arm, had taken a stab at it differently.

'I think it says *"The Italians are all relaxed and friendly"*, Miss.'

Terrific. Goal! He'd earned a flash of Miss Arnott's wonderful smile, and been sent back to his desk in a riot of applause, weighed down by his gleaming halo.

Yes, hunches could work. It was just a pity that, tonight, they'd lost those precious minutes going back to blot out that comma thing. And Wayne hadn't speeded matters up by doing his *Hunchback of Notre Dame* both ways down the corridor. But what took the most time, and landed Simon with his punishment circuits, was finding somewhere safe to put the flour babies.

Wayne was for shoving them behind the cistern pipes.

'No one will see them here,' he'd called down from where he was perched, on a lavatory stall partition.

'Throw them up, Sime.'

Furtively, Simon unwrapped Wayne's flour baby from the spare shirt in which he'd hidden it, and passed it up. Wayne was about to wedge it between the pipes when Simon suddenly asked him:

'Are you sure it's clean?'

Wayne blinked down like an owl caught in a torch's glare.

'Clean?'

'Yes. Are the pipes clean?'

'Grief, Sime!'

But already Simon was stepping on the lavatory seat and hoisting himself up on the partition beside Wayne. He ran his finger along the lower of the two pipes.

'It's filthy! It needs a good wipe.'

'Sime! Don't be a plague-spot! We're already late!'

'It'll only take a minute.'

Slithering down the partition wall, Simon dived under the nearest sink, in search of a cloth.

'Sime ...'

'Hold on, Wayne. There must be a cloth somewhere round here.'

'Sime! Pass my dolly thing up! Now!'

'I don't believe this! Ten lavs, ten sinks, and no cloth! I mean, I'm not fussy, but wouldn't you think –'

'That's it, Sime!'

Wayne let himself down to the floor, picked up his flour baby, scrambled back up, and shoved it tight between the pipes.

'It'll get *filthy*, Wayne.'

Wayne wasn't listening. Rubbing the grime on his fingers off on to his tracksuit, he made for the door.

'Bye, Sime! Enjoy your press-ups!'

Simon lifted his own flour baby out of his sports bag.

'Come on, sweetheart,' he told her. 'Let's go outside where it smells less hoofy. We'll find you somewhere nice to sit, in the fresh air.'

The place he chose was a bush a few yards behind the one goal still flooded in sunlight. He thrust the flour baby into the rather meagre greenery, desperately hoping she would appear to be no more than a bundle of towel to the circle of his team mates already booting the ball to one another in the warm-up. Mr Fuller was watching him dangerously, arms folded, from the side of the pitch. But still Simon took his time, wedging the flour baby firmly into the bush. Mr Fuller was the least of his problems. At least now the snoopers couldn't pick on him. She was there, in sight, and she was clean and safe. Mr Fuller could punish him for being late by giving him fifty press-ups. But if Simon got thrown off the flour baby project, he might miss The Glorious Explosion.

And it was going to be *brilliant*. That much he knew. Once or twice since Mr Cartright dealt out the flour babies, Simon had suffered moments of doubt. It struck him that he might somehow have misheard the conversation in the staffroom, or missed the point. And even if he hadn't, one question still remained to be answered. Was the whole business worth it? After all, it wasn't generally Simon's way to stick at a project for the length of a lesson, let alone for a whole three weeks. Would any – *could* any explosion Mr Cartright had to offer be worth the grind of dragging this flour baby around, keeping her clean, for twenty-one days of his life?

Yes. Yes, it could and would. Hadn't he heard that from the expert himself, Dr Feltham? Running to join the warm-up, Simon braced himself against the look on Mr Fuller's face by remembering what had happened that very afternoon, in the school corridor. He played it through his brain one more time, like a favourite moment on video. Mr Cartright had been beached up on the radiator outside the classroom door, seemingly doing nothing more strenuous than admiring the knot in his laces. It looked the picture of an unofficial break: the teacher idling outside in the corridor, the class causing mayhem within. But anyone who had strolled back late to Miss Arnott's class last year as often as Simon knew the set-up for what it was. Mr Cartright, wasn't resting. He was listening. In fact, he was about to pounce. What he was doing out there in the corridor was taking a moment to work out to which of the hoodlums inside he would most enjoy awarding a punishment essay.

Simon was accustomed to this old routine. At any moment, Mr Cartright would heave his great carcass off the radiator shelf, sidle softly to the door, take a deep breath, and let it out on the other side in such a bellow that poor Miss Arnott, in the next door room, would all but fall off her chair from fright.

Simon slid back round the corner and waited. From Carthorse's point of view, he reckoned, the fewer punishment essays to dish out the better. Like Simon, he was not a great reader. If Simon showed himself now, he'd be bound to become Carthorse's prey in an instant. But wait till some other poor victim had been named, and Simon might get a home run through the doorway and back to his desk in all the riot of somebody else's 'Who? *Me*, sir? Sir! Why *me?* It isn't fair!'

Worth the risk, anyway.

Simon lounged against the wall, waiting. And that was how he came to see Dr Feltham and his retinue of willing helpers ('crawlers' to Simon), coming round the bend in the corridor. Piled in their arms were all the complicated and unwieldy bits of equipment without which it seemed Dr Feltham couldn't get through a single forty-minute period in the last weeks before his great Science Fair.

Simon doubled up in a fake coughing fit. Dr Feltham and his retinue swept past. And Simon stopped coughing just in time to catch Dr Feltham's remark as he strode past his colleague, still parked on the radiator.

'Starting the term with a real bang, I see, Eric.'

Mr Cartright dealt Dr Feltham one of his poisonous looks, but Simon's doubts were banished and his worries fled away. After all, Dr Feltham was famous for his extraordinary detonations. His exploding custard tins were the envy of all. If someone with his credentials could admire in advance any big bang of Mr Cartright's, then that had to settle it once and for all. The experiment was going to be glorious.

Simon's smile widened into rapture then. And now, as he booted the football across the circle to Wayne, it was widening again. It was, thought Simon, a bit like one of those promises God used to make to those people he'd been spatting with in the Old Testament ... a covenant! They'd done a whole module on them in first year. Rainbows, floods, dead babies – that sort of thing. Well, Dr Feltham coming down the corridor and saying what he did just as Simon happened to be standing there was a sort of covenant in itself. A private promise between The Explosion and Simon ...

Mr Fuller materialized beneath his left elbow.

'I see we're in blinkers today,' he started pleasantly enough as Simon, startled, bungled the next pass. 'Not wearing a watch, though, were we?'

No point in *saying* anything, thought Simon. All that would happen is that Mr Fuller would pitch into some fresh complaint about him leaving his underwear trailed over the local greenery. And then the flour baby might catch it.

Simon pawed the ground apologetically with his boot, and said nothing. Fortunately, just at that moment Froggie Hines and Saul Epstein collided with one another, and rolled over and over, inextricably tangled.

Mr Fuller sentenced Simon on the trot.

'Three full circuits at the end, please. And *tickling* the ball, not booting it!'

He turned his foghorn voice on to the other two.

'Hines! Get your foot out of his ear'ole! Get *up*, boy! Fetch that ball!'

Simon took off for the safety of the back line while the going was good. He'd escaped press-ups, at least. And the rest of the practice wasn't too bad, what with one short break while Fruzzy Woods was seriously bawled out for waving through the hedge at his girlfriend Lucinda, and another a few minutes later when Mr Fuller caught sight of Lucinda for a second time, and held up the next throw-in while he gave her an earful.

So having to stay and dribble the ball three times round the pitch after everyone else had gone back to the changing rooms shouldn't have been too much of a pain. Of course he was missing a good laugh: Froggie's look of sheer wonder when he picked up his tin of foot powder, and, egged on by Wayne, read its vastly inflated claim. But Simon could easily imagine his face. And Wayne would fill him in on details later. So why was he making such a hash of the circuits? Why weren't his feet under his control?

Boot … Boot … Boot … Boot …

'What *are* you thinking about, lad? Don't hammer it! Treat it gentle as a baby!'

Mr Fuller's talk of babies made it worse. Rattled, Simon glanced back over his shoulder at the bush he'd just run past. Was that the right one? Where was the flour baby? Was the little sack of her still propped up safely in the branches, or had the lads noticed as they thundered off the field? Maybe Wayne had even split on him! Was she still there, all wrapped up and happy as a sandboy, or had they reached in and dug her out? Were they kicking her around the changing rooms right now, having another good laugh pretending she was a football?

Froggie would kick her hardest. She'd be *destroyed*.

Distracted, Simon missed the ball entirely.

The bellow came over the pitch on cue.

'Are you trying to be funny, Simon Martin? You certainly aren't amusing me!'

He nearly missed again. This was unreal. These weren't even proper kicks. He was only dribbling. And yet he couldn't concentrate at all. How were you supposed to get your feet going in the right directions when your brain was totally cluttered up with horror-show visions of what might be happening to your flour baby? It was a pity Mr Fuller was watching him so closely, or he could spin round, dancing on his toes, and take a proper look at the bush. The flour baby was bound to be in there still, all safely bundled up. It's just he could concentrate better if he was *sure*.

Unwilling to bring the wrath of Mr Fuller down on his head again, Simon didn't turn. He kept his face forward and ran, as one ghastly vision after another swam through his brain. His flour baby floating, face down in one of the scummy sinks, then gradually sinking as the water soaked through her thin sacking! Froggie borrowing a felt pen and, with their unauthorized alterations to his tin of foot-powder in mind, taking sweet revenge on her face with some artwork: a nose, a gappy smile, two cauliflower ears – worse! And, most disastrous of all, Jimmy Holdcroft drawing back his foot as she lay so vulnerably on the changing room floor, about to demonstrate his vicious and spectacular goal kick.

Simon hurled himself onwards. Is this, he asked himself, what people go through every time they leave a baby sitting in a pram outside a shop? No wonder they always looked so grim, pushing and shoving in their hurry to get out again. No wonder you kept crashing into them, on escalators and in doorways, determinedly hauling pushchairs where pushchairs obviously couldn't go.

His foot missed the ball again, and it rolled past.

'I'm watching you like a hawk, Simon Martin! Keep up this performance and you'll be doing press-ups afterwards!'

Ten yards to the corner. And then, at last, he would be able to swivel his head and see the bush out of the corner of his eye. One thing he'd learned, it was ridiculous trying to practise football and watch a flour baby. No one can do two things properly at the same time. Weren't they always saying that? 'You can't be concentrating on your work if you're staring out of that window!' And, 'No one can talk and listen simultaneously. If you're talking, you're not listening.' It was one of their regular, all-purpose naggings.

And his mum was exactly the same. 'You can't do your homework properly with that radio blaring, Simon.' Or,

'Make toast or play with the dog – one or the other, but not both. That's the fourth slice of bread that's gone up in flames!' She knew he couldn't do two things at once. None of this would have happened if she'd offered to look after the flour baby for him. She'd brought him up all by herself, after all. She must know what it was like. She must have realized that his football practice would turn into total disaster. Had she forgotten all those evenings she took him with her to the club while she played badminton? They were wretched enough. He still remembered peeling the back of his legs off those horrible plastic bucket seats again and again, in order to drape himself over the balcony, and call down:

'Can we go home now, please?'

Over and over, the same answer floated up from the court.

'Be patient, Simon. We're nearly finished.'

He'd sit there for what seemed another fifteen hours, bored out of his skull, and then ask:

'Can I go on ahead, Mum?'

'Simon, please! I won't be much longer. This is the last game.'

Maybe it was. But as soon as they finished playing it, Mum's partner Sue would always act as if Simon's misery and restlessness was just something best ignored, like gnats or rain, and sweep his mother along to the club room for her idea of 'just one quick drink'. If Simon so much as opened his mouth to complain, he was treated to an earful along with his coca-cola.

'Simon, please! It was a hard game, and I'm thirsty. We'll only be a few minutes. Try and be patient.'

He'd sit in a separate booth, sullenly stirring the bubbles out of his drink with his straw while she and Sue gassed away: 'Her husband ...' 'My father ...' 'Their neighbours ...' 'His daughter ...' He'd glance round the club room for the ninetieth time. No one his age. No one to stand beside at the machines. No one to muck about with in the lavatories.

He'd hang over the partition between their two booths.

'Why can't I stay home by myself?'

'Soon, sweetheart. As soon as you're old enough.'

'I could have a babysitter.'

'Simon! It's once a week! For one hour! You know this is practically the only time I ever get to go out. Now don't be a pain!'

And he'd been nine or ten. She didn't even have to watch out for him. He wasn't going to fall out of a bush and get covered in mud, or be kidnapped and kicked to bits in the changing rooms ...

Round the last corner! He could see the worst! Was that really the flour baby, still safely hidden in the bush? Did the bundle of towel look as bulky as when he first stuffed it in there? Or had – ?

Once more the ball rolled between his feet, unchecked.

'I'm warning you, Martin! One more duff yard, and you'll be following this with fifty press-ups!'

It wasn't a job for one person, that was the truth of it. To look after a flour baby, you needed two. A substitute. A reserve. Someone with no particular plans for the evening. He'd heard his mother saying as much often enough herself when she couldn't find a babysitter, or they couldn't afford one. It would have been a whole lot easier if there'd been two of them, that was for sure. Odd, then, to realize he'd never heard her wishing his father back again (unless you counted the time she'd stood at the end of his bed and said rather sourly: 'So. Mumps. Pity your father's not here to look after you ...')

But Simon had missed him. Oh, not personally. It wasn't possible to miss someone whom you'd never known, and whose face was a rather blurry picture. The person Simon missed was someone he had made up. Dark and curly-haired, as in the few poor photos he'd found lying about in drawers. And with a splendid singing voice, as even Gran still admitted. 'A glorious tenor. When he sang out, he made the rafters ring.' But it was Simon who threw in the crinkly blue eyes and the strong hands, the grin and the genius at throwing and catching. Long hours of Simon's childhood had been spent working out how his father would come back. One day he'd change his mind. He'd just show up, without any warning, and he and Mum would try again. And this time it would work. He'd want to stay. As Simon sauntered down Wilberforce Road each afternoon on his way back from his first school, he'd let his thoughts run riot around his father. He would be standing at the gate, his arms outstretched. He'd shout to hurry Simon. And Simon's run would shake the paving stones under his feet, till finally he made it past the last house, and hurled himself into those strong arms.

Ten feet from the corner, Simon would slow his pace, to hold the dream a few moments longer. Then, just as he'd conjured his dad up, he'd snuff him out. Wipe him away, before turning into his own street. It was a trick he learned to keep disappointment from rising, like tears, and spoiling the pleasure of getting home.

He'd cried once, though. He hadn't been able to help it. He'd been terribly young – only about six, for heaven's sake. Six-year-olds cried all the time. He had the main part in the Christmas play. (Joseph the car-painter, as he thought at first, till Miss Ness put him straight.) He'd learned his words, and had a scarlet cloak that trailed behind him so importantly that Miss Ness kept saying she ought to take it off him and give it to one of the three kings instead. Each time he wrapped it around himself, he could practically hear trumpets. He waited for the big day in a blaze of excitement.

And then Mum didn't come. He knew she might not, because, when she begged Mrs Spicer to walk him to school that morning, she was already unsteady on her feet, and coughing horribly. Her eyes were streaming. But through the morning he must have managed to convince himself that she would get there somehow, ill or not, because when the moment came, and Miss Ness pushed him out on to the stage, the first thing he'd done was peer along the rows of faces, desperate to find her.

'I'll be right beside the door if I make it,' she'd promised him.

And there was Sue. Funny – he'd never realized before that Mum must have dragged herself downstairs to phone Sue at the last minute. And Sue must have dropped everything – taken a whole afternoon off work and rushed across town – just to be sitting where Mum told her, right beside the door, trying to be someone for him.

It wasn't the same, though. And during the short break between the scenes, Miss Ness, struggling with Hyacinth's huge foil star, forgot for an instant.

'Never mind,' she'd said. 'Is your dad there?'

The moment the words were out of her mouth, she realized her mistake. But it was too late. He was in floods of tears. She pulled him on her knee and patted him. But it was no good. The tears were rolling and they wouldn't stop. In the end, too many minutes had gone by. The interval couldn't last for ever. So Simon had to let her unpin his glorious scarlet cloak and wrap it round Hamid, who had been boasting about knowing everyone's lines from the very first day they had started.

Boot!

He gave the ball a savage kick.

'There you go, Dad,' he panted. 'That one's for not being there.'

He kicked even harder.

'Ever!'

Boot! Boot! Boot!

He could hear Mr Fuller thundering up behind him, but he couldn't care.

Boot! Boot!

'That's it, Simon Martin! I've had *enough.*'

BOOT!

Reaching the last stretch, Simon drew back his foot and gave the ball such an almighty kick that it went flying over the roof of the changing rooms.

'That one's for you, Dad,' he shouted. 'Thanks for *nothing*!'

He realized afterwards that he was grateful for the punishment. After all, he was more than fit enough to add on fifty press-ups. The extra effort even dulled the pain. But, best of all, they took a bit of time. Not much more than two or three minutes, even taking them steadily and doing them properly. But long enough – almost exactly long enough – to give the fierce glittering in his eyes time to subside.

Notes for Chapter 5

In this chapter we see the public faces and private worlds of teachers and pupils. We are allowed inside Miss Arnott's thoughts and see her mixed opinions of Simon Martin. Similarly, as he sits in detention writing his flour baby diary, Simon exposes his thoughts about his father, which Miss Arnott reads over his shoulder. In the meantime, Sajid is looking at the flour baby problem from a commercial angle.

What do you think?
As you read through, think about the personalities of the teachers you are shown. Do you think Miss Arnott is a likeable and realistic character?

Questions
1. Dr Feltham is pleased to see Simon is learning from his diary entries. What else has Simon learnt about teachers and students by the middle of this chapter?
2. Miss Arnott obviously finds Simon a lively and bright character. Pick three words or phrases from her thoughts on him that reflect this.
3. What kind of person is Sajid? Think of three words to describe his character and support them with quotations from the text.
4. Why do you think Anne Fine chooses not to make Simon change his personality and become one of the 'ear'oles' at the end of this chapter? Which would you rather he did?

Further activities
1. With a partner try to make a list of common errors that young people make in their writing. Think about spelling, punctuation and grammar.

Then, individually, write out one of Simon's diary entries with 12 deliberate mistakes. Swap your work with someone else in the class and mark it, as if you were either Mr Cartright or Dr Feltham, with a teacher comment at the end.

2. Research information about the following people's diaries: Adrian Mole, Samuel Pepys, Anne Frank, Bridget Jones. Which of these diaries would you find in the library under fiction and which would you find under non-fiction?

Chapter 5

'Is this really the sort of thing you had in mind?'

Ambushed on his way out of the staff lavatories, Dr Feltham flicked through the sheaf of pages Mr Cartright had thrust in his hand.

'Go on,' urged Mr Cartright. 'Read one.'

Dr Feltham glanced, puzzled, at the name scrawled across the grubby sheet of paper on the top.

'Simon Martin? Isn't he one of mine?'

'No, he isn't,' snapped Mr Cartright. 'The one you have is called Martin Simon. You must know the boy – passes exams, reads Baudelaire – that sort of thing. This one is Simon Martin. One of mine. Spends half his time skulking in the lavatories, and the other half shuffling round acting a stick short of the full bundle.'

Dr Feltham couldn't help rebuking his colleague for his unprofessional way of speaking.

'I think you mean, Eric, that he's not yet living up to his full academic potential.'

'Just what I said,' insisted Mr Cartright. 'Goes about behaving like a half-wit.'

Less than three feet away, behind the door of the boys' lavatories, Simon Martin sank on his heels and buried his head in his hands as Dr Feltham ploughed through the joint obstacles of crabbed writing and pitiful spelling, to read aloud the first page of his flour baby diary.

I think the whole idea of carrying a flour baby around is completely stupid because she doesn't even cry, or eat anything, or mess any nappies.

Still, mine has been a total drag all day.

I thought my mother was a real meanie for not looking after her for a measly two hours while I did football. After all, she's had enough practice looking after people. She's looked after me for 122,650 hours, if Foster's calculator works all right. And apparently I was quite noisy, and ate a lot, and made huge messes. Maybe that's why my dad only managed to stick a pathetic 1008 hours. Foster says that makes him 121.6765 times more of a meanie than my mum, but I reckon Foster may have pressed some of the wrong buttons.

When it came, Dr Feltham's response was even more of a shock to Simon than it was to Mr Cartright.

'But this is splendid, Eric! Absolutely splendid! Look what the lad's learned already. On only the first day he's grasped that, even freed from three of the principal disadvantages of parenthood, the responsibilities are *immense.* He's learned a little about his own early childhood development. And he's even branched out into some quite sophisticated arithmetical calculations, working in tandem with this Foster.'

Behind the door, Simon lifted his head from his hands, and stared at the wall in astonishment. Could he be hearing right? Was this *praise?*

Outside, Dr Feltham glanced again at the laboriously written page.

'Interesting that he already thinks of his sack of flour as female. What do you make of that, Eric?'

But, too excited to wait for Mr Cartright's opinion on the matter, he went on to decode Simon's second page.

DAY 2

Today Macpherson got a funny look in his eye, grabbed my flour baby, and gave her a bit of a chew down the bottom of our garden. Mum says I am lucky our dog has such clean slobber and most of it came off.

If I ever have a real baby, I will certainly make sure it gets all its shots against rabies.

I am watching Macpherson very carefullly indeed.

Dr Feltham waved the page in the air.

'See?' he crowed to Mr Cartright. 'See, Eric? On the second day he's learning about the staining capacity of canine salivary exudate on woven organic material –'

'Slobber on sacking!'

In his enthusiasm, Dr Feltham failed to catch Mr Cartright's tone of outright scorn.

'Exactly so!' he agreed. 'Not only that, but he's already begun to reflect on the vital importance of primary childhood inoculation.'

He stabbed the sheet of paper with his forefinger.

'For all we know, Eric, this lad may already have gone to the trouble of looking up the first presenting symptoms of rabies. How else would he know what to watch for in Macpherson?'

Behind the door, the look on Simon's face was turning from bewilderment to pride. It wasn't often that his work was praised. In fact, now he came to think about it, he couldn't recall it ever happening before. Maybe he should have stayed in Dr Feltham's class, where he might have been properly appreciated. It was a shame that interfering ear'ole Martin Simon had come along and bounced him out of there on the first morning. What did it matter which way round you wrote your name? Martin Simon. Simon Martin. What was the difference, anyway?

Buoyed with fresh confidence, Simon rocked on his heels in happy expectation while Dr Feltham rustled his way through the loose sheets of paper, searching for the third page of his diary.

DAY 3

Today Hooper got hold of my flour baby for a bit of a muck-about so I called him an animal and stamped on his sandwiches. Then Mr Cartright puffed in, saving my flour baby from doom and giving us both a detention.

Not me and the flour baby. Me and Hooper.

Behind the door, Simon lowered his gaze to the tiled floor. For the first time in his life, he regretted not having tried just that little bit harder, done that little bit more. He felt somehow he'd let Dr Feltham down. And through the door he heard with a twinge of shame the disappointed tones:

'A lot less learned yesterday, admittedly. But never mind, Eric. We shall have to content ourselves with hoping the lad makes the very best use of his detention.'

His footfalls faded down the corridor, punctuated only by Mr Cartright's resonant snort of contempt, as he took off in the other direction. Simon crept out. The pile of flour baby reports, he saw, had been dumped on the radiator shelf. Unwilling to go straight along to the detention room and risk his reputation by arriving on time, Simon lounged against the wall, leafing through them.

He found Sajid's the easiest to read because he'd already heard the story in the cloakroom, several times, and that gave him a good start.

DAY 3

I took my flour baby on the bus today. It was shoved under my arm, out of the way, till some interfering old trout forced me to sit down and put it on my lap. All the way down the Foleshill Road she kept poking it and nattering to it. I thought she was a loony. But when we reached the bus stop at the Eye Centre, she got off.

I hope my eyes never go that bad.

Russ Mould's was underneath. Simon did have a stab at trying to decipher the first few words. But it turned out to be harder than one of those '*Unscramble these letters to find the names of five vegetables'* quiz books his mum used to waste her time and money buying him before the long bus journey to Gran's house.

In the end he gave up, and turned to Rick Tullis's effort. He found this one surprisingly easy to read, perhaps because he and Tullis obviously shared a trick or two, both in handwriting and in spelling.

DAY 1

I said I wasn't coming in if we did babies, and if Mr Henderson hadn't spotted me down the shops I wouldn't be here today. I definitely shan't be here tomorrow. Or the next day. Or –

Suddenly recalling that the minimum number of sentences for the daily entry was three, Rick Tullis had broken off promptly at this point, considering duty done.

Simon ran his eyes a second time over Tullis's brief and sullen report. Perhaps he was still warmed by Dr Feltham's generous praise. Perhaps the glimpse of insight came spontaneously. But, staring at Rick Tullis's niggardly and mean-spirited scribblings, Simon saw for the first time why teachers showed such scorn for those who did as little as possible. He understood why lesson after lesson was shot through with their howls of exasperation and anguish.

'Believe me, George Spalder, it's not *me* who's the poorer for your not bothering to do your homework. It's you.'

'To me, Tullis, this blank page signifies just one more piece of paper I don't have to take home and mark. To you, on the other hand, it signifies yet another blank patch in your brain.'

'I know I didn't specifically say *you* had to do it, Luis. I'm not in the habit of saying "Everyone has to do the work, and that also goes for Luis Pereira".'

Suddenly it all *meant* something to Simon. He was struck by the sheer grit of teachers. Their stout hearts. Their unflagging fixity of purpose. Determinedly they bashed on, term after term, trying to make their pupils give their very best. And with what results? With what thanks? Simon was appalled to think how often he (and so many others) had insulted these dedicated saints in human form by handing in such shoddy work. How *could* he have been so ungrateful? How *could* he?

There and then, Simon vowed to make amends. He would begin by fulfilling Dr Feltham's fond hope that he'd make the best use of his time in the detention room. Resolutely, he shovelled the pile of flour baby reports back on the radiator shelf, scooped up his book bag and strode off down the corridor, not even stopping to draw one or two tiny cartoon figures on this week's wall display, as usual.

Hearing the door shudder horribly on its hinges, Miss Arnott looked up. When she saw it was Simon Martin she couldn't help sighing. She'd had him in detention often enough before, and, unacquainted with his change of heart, all that went through her mind was that his arrival presaged, as usual, a farewell to quiet marking, an end to peace.

She leaned back in her chair and waited for the performance. What would it be for starters? A swipe at Hooper with the book bag, of course, just to remind him of his joint role in whatever villainy it was that had landed them there in the first place.

Then to warm up, perhaps, the drama of the pencil. Its noisy and argumentative borrowing, followed, in natural order, by its sharpening, its dropping with a clatter, its ostentatious chasing across the floor and its resharpening, then the flicking of its broken point at one of the window panes. Hearing the *ping*, Miss Arnott would be expected to raise her head in time to watch the pencil finally being used – as a drumstick for the tattoo on the desk top.

Unless, today, he chose to stage one of her favourite entertainments: the Bloodied Tongue. Last time she supervised Simon Martin, he had gone to some trouble and effort to suck enough ink out of his pen cartridge to stain his tongue bright red. He'd let this gory-looking monstrosity hang out of his mouth for the whole of the rest of the detention, quite putting her off her sandwich but amusing her mightily. Miss Arnott secretly hoped she might be treated to the Bloodied Tongue again today.

Though what she liked most of all was his Rip Van Winkle.

She found that tremendously soothing. Simon would sprawl over the desk, give a few gargantuan yawns, and then appear to fall into a sleep so deep no one could wake him for a hundred years. From time to time (whenever he feared that she'd forgotten him), he'd snore: a gentle faraway ripple that swelled ever richer and deeper, until each lungful of air that he released was reverberant enough to set the window frames rattling. Just as she began to fear for the structure of the building, he'd let out a giant snort and pretend that he'd woken himself. He'd stare around blankly, smacking his lips like an old man. And then he'd settle back down on the desk, and replay the whole performance from start to finish.

Yes. Rip Van Winkle was her favourite. The act she didn't like was Gibbering Idiot. She'd seen it too often and was bored with it. He'd sit at his desk, making grotesque faces. Every now and again he'd erupt into fits of maniacal laughter or frantic bursts of muttering. Sometimes he drooled. She hoped it wasn't going to be the Gibbering Idiot. But, just in case, Miss Arnott reached in her bag, to check that she still had her aspirins.

And her hand froze. Before her eyes – was she dreaming? was this really happening? – young Simon Martin crossed the room, ignoring Hooper totally. He drew out the chair behind the desk furthest away from the three other malefactors she was watching, pulled his flour baby, a pad of paper and a pen from his book bag, and, without making any fuss, propped the flour baby up on the desk top, patted her head affectionately once or twice, then settled straight down to work.

Miss Arnott blinked.

'Simon?' she whispered. 'Simon, are you all right?'

He looked up.

'Excuse me?'

It sounded almost like a mild rebuke, as if she'd interrupted him in an important train of thought.

'I was just wondering if you were all right.'

He stared at her.

'Yes. I'm all right. Why?'

She shook her head.

'No reason.'

And for the life of her, she couldn't think of any. Except that it wasn't *normal*. Well, it was normal, of course. But that was exactly what was wrong. With Simon Martin, acting normal wasn't normal.

Maybe the lad was sick – feverish, perhaps. Or maybe he was in shock. It's possible he'd just heard his mother had been knocked down by a lorry, or electrocuted changing a plug, or drowned in a canal, or –

Miss Arnott tried to pull herself together and dismiss the lurid flow of her imagination. Surely a pupil should be able to sit down quietly and get on with a bit of written work without one of his teachers presuming he needed an ambulance, or his mother was already inside one!

She tried to go back to her marking. But it was impossible. She couldn't concentrate at all. She kept having to raise her eyes from the books, and check on Simon Martin. What was he writing so industriously? He seemed to be covering whole sheets of paper. She'd taught him English for two whole years, and in all that time she never once saw him cover half a page in less than a double period. Who or what could have inspired the boy to scribble away so busily today?

Miss Arnott had to know. Slipping from the desk, she crept round the room on her rubber soles, till she was directly behind him. She leaned forward a little, so she could see over his shoulder. And with two years of decoding the work of Russ Mould in her professional armoury, Miss Arnott no longer had any problem at all deciphering Simon's crabbed writing and his unique spelling forms.

DAY 4

Till I was forced to lug this stupid flour baby round with me everywhere I go, I never thought about my dad having to look after me. When I asked Mum, she said he wasn't too bad at it really. He never dropped me on my head, or left me floating face down in the bath while he went off for a towel, or anything like that.

It's just he didn't stay.

I've asked why he left before. Mum and Gran always say it didn't have anything to do with me, it wasn't my fault, and it was bound to have happened anyway. But last night I asked Mum how he left, and when she tried to fob me off as usual, I wouldn't let her.

Simon broke off. He wasn't sure how to describe the next bit. Mum had rolled up her eyes, the way she always did when she was getting fed up with a conversation.

'How many times do I have to say it, Simon? I don't *know* why he left.'

'But I'm not asking *why*. I'm asking *how*.'

'How?'

'Yes. How? How did he go? What did he *say*? What did *you* say? Was there a giant great row? Was Gran there?'

He leaned across the table.

'I'm not asking you to tell me what was inside his *brain*. I'm asking something different.'

She was close to defeat. He knew it, and pressed his advantage home.

'I have a right to know.'

She reached over the table and patted his hand.

'I know, I know.'

But she said nothing more. So Simon pushed on. 'You've finished with *him*, right? And he's definitely finished with *us*. He's disappeared, never sent any money, and never even written. I bet, after all this time, even a private detective couldn't find him.'

He pulled his fingers out from under her hand.

'But *I'm* not quite finished with *him*. See? There's things I think about. Things I want to know. And this is one of them.'

He stared down at his battered knuckles, close to tears.

'Please, Mum. Tell me about the day he left.'

And so she told him – told him everything – right down to what his father had for breakfast that morning, and what he was wearing, and even the rude things he said about the people in the next flat when their dog started barking at the postman as usual. She told him all the things his father did that morning, and what they had for lunch. She even remembered the joke he made to Sue when she came round, about needing her regular Saturday afternoon fix of cuddling the baby.

'Me.'

'You.'

She spread her hands, like someone trying to convince a policeman of her innocence.

'Honestly, Simon,' she said. 'Nothing was different. There wasn't anything about the day to make it special. So far as anyone could make out afterwards, your dad wasn't in a mood, or feeling jealous or left out, or anything. In fact, when he disappeared, everyone thought that something terrible must have happened – a road accident or something. It was only afterwards we worked out that some time in the afternoon he must have packed the large blue bag and lowered it out of one of the back windows on a rope. When he strolled out of the gate, he wasn't carrying a thing. He had his hands in his pockets and he was whistling. We thought he was going to buy beer, or a bar of chocolate or something. But he must have walked round to the back of the building, picked up his bag, and gone to the bus station – timing it perfectly for the last coach to London.'

She gave a rueful smile.

'As soon as she heard that, of course, your Gran went *wild*.'

And now Simon couldn't help smiling as well. He could

imagine it. Gran down the phone on the day her son-in-law did a major bunk.

'Volcanic!'

His mother took the opportunity to rise from the table. Clearly she was hoping the conversation was over.

Simon called her attention back, just for a moment.

'What was he whistling?'

She turned and stared.

He asked again.

'What was he whistling? When he strolled out of the gate with his hands in his pockets, what tune was he whistling?'

She shook her head.

'Oh, Simon! How should I remember that?'

He didn't push his luck saying so, but for the life of him he couldn't see why it was any more strange than remembering whether a man had cornflakes or bran mix the day he walked out of the gate and down the street and out of your life for ever. Surely the tune he was whistling was far more important. It might, after all, be a clue to what he was thinking.

And what would someone only a very few years older than Simon himself have in his mind as he walked out to begin his life all over again, somewhere different. What would he be whistling? 'Faraway Roamer?' 'Long and Lonesome Road?' 'Goin' to the City and Ain't Never Comin' Back?'

And now, in the stuffy detention room, the tunes he'd thought of came back, one by one, and idled through his mind as his pen tracked over the paper, steadily setting down in his flour baby diary everything his mother had told him the night before. When little snatches of song broke through his clenched teeth in a soft whistling, Miss Arnott didn't bother to hush him. He wasn't trying to disturb the others, after all. He didn't even seem to realize he was doing it. And while he was so absorbed, she could keep making her quiet circuits of the room, and coming up behind to peep over his shoulder and read the last few sentences he'd written.

And what was strangest of all the things Mum said was that my father wasn't even cheesed off or in a mean mood that day. Somehow that makes it seem as if he wasn't so much leaving us as moving on to whatever it was he wanted next. And I've realized something else. I've realized that, if I hadn't been there, already born, my dad would by now be just one of those old boyfriends that Mum's forgotten completely. If they hadn't had me between them, she probably wouldn't even get his name right by now, let alone remember what he looked like and what he ate for breakfast. I just wish I knew what he was whistl –

The bell rang.

Miss Arnott jumped back so, when they all swivelled in their seats to look at her hopefully, Simon wouldn't realize she'd been reading his work.

'Is that it?'

'Yes. Off you go.'

He wasn't as quick as usual at stuffing his things in his bag, and making for the door. Miss Arnott took the chance to speak to him.

'Simon —'

He turned.

She didn't know quite how to put it without insulting him. In the end, she just said companionably:

'You wrote an awful lot today.'

He shrugged.

She tried again.

'Sometimes people just take time to get started with schoolwork. Late bloomers, we call them. They muck about for years, not really seeing the point of any of it. And then one day light dawns, and they actually begin to enjoy it.'

She waited.

Simon said nothing.

She knew she might as well drop it. But out of sheer, burning curiosity, she couldn't help trying one last time.

'Do you think that might be what's happened to you today?'

Simon inspected his huge feet. He didn't actually regret putting his energy into his work for the whole of the period she'd been watching him. But most of the early enthusiasm, and all of the guilt, had drained away now. He felt like an empty pen cartridge, used and spent. Just for a moment he did consider the idea of trying to stay a new person, a born-again Simon, religiously doing his homework and handing it in on time, spending his lunch hours in the library, discussing study projects in depth with his teachers. After all, the last forty minutes hadn't been too bad. His hand was aching, yes. And there was a red patch on the side of his finger where he'd been gripping the pen (though that was nothing compared with the battering he took for granted in ten minutes' football). No, what Simon didn't like – stronger than that, what he *hated* – about the last forty minutes was that they'd gone. Gone for ever. Snap! Just like that! And he'd been concentrating so hard, he hadn't even noticed them going. For forty minutes he'd been behaving like one of those ear'oles in all the other classes – the sort who might look up from the last page of the book they were reading, and be astonished that it had gone dark.

No. Your whole life could go down the drain that way if you didn't keep a look-out. You had to be very much on your guard.

Miss Arnott was still gazing at him hopefully. And Simon had always been very fond of Miss Arnott. He didn't want to be the one to crush her starry-eyed teacher's dream.

Shuffling his feet, he made a real effort to be diplomatic.

'Possibly,' he said. And then again, with a little more firmness: 'Possibly.'

And to keep her from harrying him further, he made for the door as quickly as possible.

Outside in the corridor, Simon found himself pinned

against the wall by what he at first took to be a miniature armoured car.

Over the top of it, Sajid was grinning like a fool.

'What's this, then?' Simon demanded. Sajid pulled back a few inches so Simon could free himself and take a better look.

'Isn't it obvious? It's a pram.'

'So why's it got eight wheels?'

Sajid rolled his eyes.

'Because it's actually two prams lashed together with some fusewire Tullis nicked for me, that's why.'

'But what's it for?'

'Flour babies.' Sajid's eyes shone. 'Look, Sime. How many flour babies do you reckon you could shove in this front pram without any falling out?'

Simon tugged his flour baby out of his book bag, and sat her at one end, like a queen.

'About ten,' he said, after a moment's reflection. 'They'd be a bit squashed, but they wouldn't fall out.'

'Exactly!' crowed Sajid. 'Ten in this one at the front and nine in this one at the back. All nineteen flour babies fit in these two prams tied together.'

'So?'

Sajid was getting impatient.

'Don't be such a dim bulb, Sime! It's a little travelling nursery. A *crèche*!'

'*Crush* more like,' Simon said.

Sajid started pushing. Rigidly lashed together as they

were, the prams were impossible to manoeuvre round the corner, and Sajid was reduced to doing a seven-point-turn under Simon's strident but unsystematic instruction.

'But that's the whole point,' he insisted, as the two of them finally took off at last down the straight. 'The more flour babies I can cram in, the more money I make.'

Simon was mystified.

'Money?'

Sajid turned to stare.

'This isn't going to be a *charity* crèche,' he told Simon sternly. 'If I'm taking responsibility, I'm taking money. That's business.'

Simon said disparagingly:

'Come off it, Sajid. No one will sign on for this. No one.'

'Oh yes, they will,' Sajid informed him cheerily. 'I've got ten names down already, and three more going home tonight to sift through their money bags and see if they can afford —'

Whoooomph!

He'd run into Dr Feltham, who was rounding the next turn in the corridor at such a speed he couldn't stop in time. Simon expected the worst. A giant ticking off. Another detention. Fifty lines. But Dr Feltham, when he caught his wind, simply prowled round the strange eight-wheeled vehicle, eyeing its visible features and weighing up its attributes.

'Extraordinary!'

He spun round to address the little crowd of acolytes

trailing behind him with their arms full of laboratory equipment.

'Extraordinary! Most fortuitous! Here we were only this morning discussing articulation in vehicles, and here in the corridor is a perfect example of exactly what I was trying to explain. Note that, with a rigid rectangular structure of these proportions and –'

Here, he broke off to peer briefly under the prams.

'Eight wheels –'

Distracted, he stopped again.

'What is this?' he asked, pointing. 'Is this thirty-amp fuse wire? I certainly hope it didn't come from any of Mr Higham's workshops!'

Then, without even waiting for an answer, he ushered his little group on, still lecturing them mightily about such mysteries as angles of approach, and separate speeds and velocities.

Simon and Sajid lounged against the wall and watched them walk away. Sajid was relieved that Tullis's theft of ten metres of fuse wire had not fully registered with Dr Feltham, and Simon was reassured that his decision not to become one of the ear'oles had been exactly the right one. Just for the moment, he felt safe again.

They watched in silence for a few more seconds. Then Sajid nudged Simon as the last of Dr Feltham's retinue disappeared round the bend in the corridor.

'Sad lives …' he said, shaking his head.

Simon echoed, 'Sad lives …'

Forcibly they shook themselves out of the mournful mood into which what little they understood of the impromptu lesson on articulation had unaccountably thrown them.

Together they pushed the pram off down the corridor to find somewhere with a steep slope, and cheer themselves up with a good laugh.

Notes for Chapter 6

Most of the boys are now tired of the responsibility that has been forced upon them through the project. The purpose of Dr Feltham's project was for the boys to learn about themselves. We can see their varying reactions to their flour babies and learn about them as characters. Simon considers the reasons why his father might have left him. He thinks about the pleasures, as well as the difficulties his father missed.

What do you think?
The boys air their frustrations about looking after their flour babies. As you read through, you can see how Anne Fine is relating these to real parenthood. Some of these young people cannot even cope with a flour baby. Consider what difficulties they would face if they had real ones!

Questions
1. Look at the simile on page 94. Why is Robin Foster described as a 'poor wounded fawn'?
2. There are several instances of italicised words in this chapter. Why does Anne Fine use them and what difference does it make when you are reading aloud?

Further activities
Slang is something that easily goes out of date, so in *Flour Babies* Anne Fine sometimes makes up her own slang.

1. Look at the words below and work out a standard English version of them. Your teacher will give you a definition of standard English if you need it.
'He couldn't imagine just <u>booting</u> her into the canal.' (page 94).
'Simon Martin had gone <u>quite daffy</u> over his bag of flour.' (page 94).
'He's had his busfare robbed by Sajid's <u>hard nuggets</u>.' (page 96).

2. Make a dictionary of your own slang. With a partner make a list of words that your peers use that older people might not understand. Write out a clear dictionary definition of each of them.

Chapter 6

On day 11, Robin Foster lost his temper and kicked his flour baby in the canal. It sank almost at once. Three days before, at the twice weekly weigh-in, things had been going well enough. His flour baby hadn't lost any weight from ill-treatment. Nor had it gained any from added damp. But on the way home from school on the eleventh day, something in Robin snapped, and the result was a few rising bubbles, and a line of curious faces peering into the filthy black water of the canal.

'Death-blow!'

'Seriously sunk, Foster!'

'You *and* the baby ...'

'Why did you *do* that?'

But Robin seemed reluctant to explain.

'I just couldn't help it, see?'

'No,' Simon said, pulling his own flour baby's bonnet straight. 'I don't see. I don't see at all.'

Robin scowled at him horribly.

'Well, maybe your flour baby is a whole lot easier to look after than mine.'

'Rubbish!' scoffed Simon, though secretly he did think that it might be true. His own flour baby had a way of watching with those big round eyes that made her easy to look after. He often found himself chatting to her companionably. 'Comfy?' he'd ask, as he propped her on top of the rest of the stuff in his book bag. 'Happy?' as he lifted her to the top of the wardrobe (the only place

Macpherson couldn't get at her). Using his flour baby to join in a Glorious Explosion was going to be difficult enough. But at the very least it would be something extraordinary, something quite awesome. He couldn't imagine just booting her in the canal.

'What made you *do* it?' he asked again.

If it had been only Simon who was curious, Robin would have ignored the question. After all, everyone in the whole school knew by now that Simon Martin had gone quite daffy over his bag of flour. But the other three were watching him as well. Gwyn Phillips had even got off his bike. Everyone was standing waiting for his answer. They were, he thought, like a pack of jackals closing in on some poor wounded fawn.

'I don't *know* why I did it,' he snapped. 'I just lost my temper, didn't I? I just got sick of the stupid thing staring at me day after day.'

'Yours didn't stare,' Simon couldn't help pointing out. 'Yours didn't have any eyes.'

Robin turned on him.

'Oh, go walk the plank, Sime! It's all right for you. You don't mind going around acting like a major wally. Nobody's going to laugh at you, are they? Nobody's going to tease someone the size of a gorilla for strolling about chucking a six-pound bag of flour under the chin, and singing it lullabies –'

'Now look here, Foster –'

But Robin was too annoyed to stop.

'It's all right for you, you great big-fisted ape. Nobody tangles with you. But what about the rest of us?'

'Yeh!'

'Too true!'

'Foster's right.'

Simon spun round to face the gang of traitors behind him.

'You're not taking *his* side?'

But it seemed they were.

Wayne Driscoll was the first to testify.

'Robin's right. I'm sick of mine, too. I'm sick of carrying it about everywhere I go, and trying to keep it dry and clean. I'm sick of the way it gets dirtier and dirtier without me even *looking* at it! I'm sick of putting it down somewhere perfectly all right for half an hour, and then, when I pick it up again, it's practically gone *black*. I tell you, I'm just about ready to boot mine in the canal as well.'

Simon tried to be reasonable.

'Why don't you put it into Sajid's crèche? He keeps them safe and clean.'

Wayne had the answer ready.

'I haven't got any *money*, have I? I'm still owing for next door's coal bin I borrowed.'

Simon tried to be patient.

'Look, Wayne,' he said. 'Luis's mother is *never* going to let him have another Haunted House party. Not after all that mess last time. You won't be using that coal bin as a coffin again for a long while. So give it back.'

'Can't, can I?' Wayne snapped. 'Not now it's bust. And anyway, if it couldn't even hold four ghouls and a vampire without falling apart at the seams, it's not going to be able to hold coal again, is it?'

His expression soured.

'That's what they're saying next door, anyhow. A new coal bin or a trip to the police station. So as well as having to clear up all the mess, I'm having to buy them a new coal bin.'

Simon was still searching for a solution.

'You could just *owe* the money to Sajid.'

This time, Wayne couldn't help laughing in his face.

'Do us a favour, Sime! If you weren't so busy cuddling your new dolly all day, you'd know that Sajid's already hired Henry and Bill to poke the money out of anyone who falls behind with their pram rent. Why do you think George is walking home with us today? He's had his busfare robbed by Sajid's hard nuggets.'

Bitterly, he tilted his head to one side and did a creditable imitation of Sajid saying, 'Very sorry, folks. That's business!'

But George was already pushing him aside in his eagerness to expand on his complaints himself.

'That's right. I'm sick of walking home. I'm sick of handing over all my money to Sajid, just to have a few measly hours off looking after this stupid thing every day. And I'm sick of getting no sympathy. Last night I was explaining how unfair it all was to my mother, and she just laughed. In fact, she said she wished Sajid had been running his pram crèche when me and my brother were babies, because she'd happily have paid double the price he charges to get rid of us for a few hours. She says this flour bag is *nothing* to the trouble and bother of a real baby. She says, when it comes to looking after things, I don't even know I'm *born*.'

His face went dark.

'I don't get hardly any money anyway. I've already had to borrow from next week's to pay Sajid last week's pram rent. I can't go on like this. By the time I give back the flour baby, I shall be months in debt. Months! I'm for kicking the thing in the canal now.'

Before Simon could argue, Gwyn Phillips had chimed in.

'Me, too! I'm fed up with mine. I'm fed up with having to tie the stupid thing safely on the back of my bike, and then go to all the extra trouble of wrapping it in a plastic bag in case some car wheel goes through a puddle and soaks it. I'm fed up with my mum and dad reminding me to take it upstairs with me every night, and bring it down again in the morning. I'm fed up with having to make sure it's never left alone in the same room as our cat. I'm ready to boot mine in the canal along with everyone else's.'

And, to prove it, he started ripping the plastic bag containing his flour baby off the back of his bike.

Simon was about to snatch it safely away when Wayne Driscoll stepped in front, holding his own flour baby ready for a drop-kick.

'Let's have a competition!' he shouted. 'See who can boot his flour baby furthest across the canal!'

'See whose sinks quickest!'

'See whose makes the most bubbles!'

Simon moved closer to the canal, spreading his arms wide, to stop them.

'*No!*'

For a moment, they turned their attention back on him.

'Don't be such a pathogen, Sime!'

'Wimpo!'

'I tell you, this flour baby business is turning you into a real *stain*.'

Simon stood his ground between the four of them and the slippery canal edge.

'Listen,' he begged. 'I know you hate them. I know you all think they're stupid and not proper Science and not worth bothering about, and you'd rather get mashed by Old Carthorse for losing them than trail them round one more day.'

He spread his hands.

'But it's going to be worth it,' he assured them. 'It is! It is! If you can just hold on –'

His eyes shone with the vision that had sustained him through eleven days.

'It's the explosion, you see,' he explained, 'It's going to be brilliant. Amazing! Like one of those things in the Bible – you know – blood rivers and plagues of frogs and locusts and first-borns, and such. I promise you, it's going to be one hundred pounds of sifted white flour exploding all over our classroom!'

'Foster's didn't explode when he booted it,' George pointed out sourly. 'Foster's just *sank*.'

Fired with the iron conviction of the religious fanatic. Simon had no trouble at all coming up with a reason to dismiss this rather inconvenient observation.

'Foster couldn't have booted it hard enough.'

Here was a challenge indeed. The little gang of them eyed one another, weakening.

Wayne was the first to crack. After all, he'd poured scorn on Robin Foster often enough in games over the last three years. And facts were facts. Robin could barely kick a ball out of a paper bag.

And it was true that, after eleven miserable days spent shackled to a flour baby, one brief booting of the thing into the canal did not match the glorious vision Simon kept holding out to them. Wayne wouldn't put money on anyone else's flour baby exploding over the water, anyway. Gwyn's goal kick was worse than Foster's. And George's was no better. Their sacks of flour would probably sink, just like Robin's, without trace. His own would explode, all right. No doubt about that. He wasn't on the football team for nothing. But even then the flour would simply blow away over the water. There wouldn't be a good and lasting mess.

No. Whichever way you looked at it, one hefty kick over the canal would not make up for eleven ruined days.

'All right,' said Wayne. 'You win. We'll wait.'

But there was still an unbeliever in their midst.

'Why?' George Spalder suddenly demanded. 'Why should we wait? Just because Sime here keeps going on and on about his wonderful explosion? You're crazy if you believe him. He must be wrong. Old Carthorse has taught in that classroom for *four hundred years*. He isn't going to let anyone kick a hundred pounds of flour about in there. He'd have to be out of his mind. No. It'll never happen. Sime must have got it all wrong.'

Simon's voice rang with honest conviction.

'It's what he *said*,' he insisted. 'I *heard* him. Don't forget I was earwigging right outside the staffroom door! 'Over a hundred pounds of sifted white flour exploding in my classroom.' That's what he *said*. His exact *words*.'

Now Wayne was torn between sense and desire.

'I don't know,' he said, scuffing the side of his shoe against a clump of grass on the tow path. 'It sounds pretty unlikely. But maybe Sime is right. After all –' His voice rose as the rigour of his thinking was suddenly overwhelmed by the strength of his feelings. After all, why else would we be forced to look after these floppy, useless, pathetic things for three whole weeks, with people snooping to make sure we do it right, if not to get us all so boiled up mad, we kick the stupid things to bits?'

He glowered round, demanding an answer.

'We were *told* why,' George Spalder reminded him. 'It's to learn about ourselves, and how we feel about the job of being a parent. That was the point.'

'Then it didn't matter me booting mine into the canal.'

Robin said cheerfully. 'Because I didn't learn anything from mine. Not one single tiny thing. I dragged that stupid bag of flour round for eleven whole days, and all I learned is that I never, *ever* want a baby in my whole life unless someone else offers to look after it at least half the day, and there's a free crèche next door!'

Everyone fell silent.

'It seems to me,' said Wayne, 'that if people had the faintest idea what a bother they were, no one would ever have a baby.'

'And,' added Robin. 'If they happened to fetch up with one by accident, anyone with any sense would run away.'

He looked to Simon for agreement. But Simon turned his back.

Then Robin realized.

With a guilty glance at the others, he reached out and laid his hand on Simon's shoulder.

Instantly, Simon shook it off, and marched back along the tow path the way they had come.

'What's up with him?' George Spalder asked, mystified.

'Shut up, you great hiccup,' whispered Robin. And he couldn't help adding importantly: 'Didn't you know Sime's dad only stuck six weeks of looking after him?'

'No,' George said. 'I didn't know that.'

He stared after Simon.

'Not very long to have a dad, is it?' he said.

Robin said portentously:

'It is exactly one thousand and eight hours.'

Everyone looked at Robin with a new respect. Then, one by one, they turned to watch in sympathy as Simon drew further and further away from them along the tow path. It was perfectly clear that he didn't want their company any longer.

Gwyn got back on his bike.

'I'll be off, then.'

George nudged Wayne. 'Come on. Let's go.' He pulled Robin along with them. 'You too, Robin. No point in hanging about here. He won't turn round and come back till we've all gone.'

And he was right. A minute or so after they disappeared between the trees on the bend, Simon glanced round to check the path was clear, and only then did he turn back again. Simon felt terrible. Unfit for company. Best left alone.

Six weeks! Six whole weeks! *Surely*, he thought, as he kicked moodily at stones along the path, six weeks was long enough! What could have been *wrong* with him as a baby? What sort of little blot could he have been, that after six whole weeks his father hadn't even thought him worth staying around for, worth bringing up? Simon had only had his flour baby eleven days, and already, just as he couldn't imagine himself simply booting her into the canal out of temper, so he couldn't think how his own father could just have walked out, whistling, one fine day. After all, Simon was *real*.

So what had been wrong with him? Simon had seen other babies. Only that morning, on the way to school, he'd practically bumped into one. It was stuffed into one of those backpacks, and its mother was standing at the kerb on the corner, waiting for the light to go green. Eleven days before, Simon could have strolled past whole swarms of babies, and not even noticed them. Now he saw every one.

It was wearing a bonnet studded with woolly knobs, with a ribbon bow under its chin. Both the baby and the bonnet looked very *clean*, Simon thought. Cheeks pink and gleaming. Wool as white as snow. He wondered how the parents managed it. For all his own studious efforts to protect her, his own flour baby seemed to be getting grubbier by the day.

As if sensing his rather envious stare, the baby turned in the backpack to look at Simon. Its ribbon chin strap slipped across its mouth, and Simon stretched out a finger, thinking to push it back.

The baby saw the finger coming. Instantly its bland pudding face was transfigured with a smile. To Simon it looked as if some mighty lightbulb had just been switched on in the baby's head. The effect was magical. The little face shone.

Simon grinned at the baby. What a doddle! To judge by the way it was beaming, you'd think Simon had just performed some absolutely unbelievable trick, some astonishing feat, like doing a treble somersault with sparklers sticking out of his ears, and not just stuck out a grubby finger.

He hooked the ribbon back under the baby's chin. It

didn't flinch. Clearly it was so amazed and thrilled by the mere sight of the finger coming close that it didn't even realize the point was to tug the bonnet straight.

Drunk with power, Simon waggled the finger.

Instantly the baby was reduced to paroxysms of mirth. It squirmed energetically in its backpack.

Its mother turned round.

'Sorry,' said Simon, and the light turned green.

All the way over the road, Simon stayed a step behind the baby, waggling his finger just above its head. The baby kicked and crowed. Simon felt quite a pang when he had to peel away on the other side. He couldn't remember ever delighting anyone so much, so easily. How old was that baby? He had no idea. He knew almost nothing about them. He did suppose that if one of those tiny, purplish newborn ones he'd seen on documentaries was put beside one of the hulking great pink ones you saw outside shops, he'd be able to tell the difference. But that was about it. Maybe, thought Simon, his dad was a duffer about babies too. Maybe, when he looked down at Simon gurgling blankly in his cot, he hadn't realized that within weeks – or was it months? – he'd turn into something like that baby at the traffic lights, who could make you feel like a million dollars, just for being able to waggle a finger.

That was the thing about babies, Simon decided. They were different from everything else. They were special. All of a sudden it was clear to him why everyone in the whole world was forever queuing up to blow raspberries on their tummies. Even if you were a complete hiccup, leading a totally sad life, a baby thought you were a real star, the best thing since sliced bread, and worth falling out of a backpack to get one last backward look at. Small wonder everyone went round saying 'Ooh!' and 'Aah!' and cooing about how much they adored them. Before, Simon had always assumed that this was simply a bit of an act, to try and cheer up the new parents. It never occurred to him for a moment that it was sincere. But now he saw people meant it. They were saying what they thought. Babies were wonderful. And it was no more than the truth. Face facts – you'd never get something that good down the shops.

And what was so good about them was that they weren't really people – not yet, anyway. And so you could treat them differently. It was easier to like them. In fact, they were a bit like pets, the way you could feed and clean and tidy up after them day after day, and even if you got cheesed off, you didn't feel they should be pulling their weight more. No one in his right mind would go all huffy because a baby wasn't doing as much for him as he was doing for the baby.

But people were a whole knottier prospect, with one side or another always feeling put upon, or taken for granted. Why, even Fruzzy Woods had got the final flick from Lucinda three days ago, for much the same sort of problem. 'I'm finished with you!' she'd yelled at him. 'I'm sick of living on a one-way street! I cheered you on in all your football matches. I even chum you to practice. And what happens when I ask you to come and support me in my badminton final? You say you haven't time!' And now, each time Fruzzy phoned her after school to beg her to come out and talk, that's all she'd say to him: 'I haven't time.'

Compared to that, loving a baby was a piece of cake. In a sudden rush of affection, Simon halted in his tracks, tugged the flour baby out of his bag, and sat down with her on his knee beside the canal.

'I'll tell you what I like about you,' he said, staring into her big round eyes. 'You're very easy to get on with. You're not like Mum, always telling me to put my plate in the sink, or shut doors more quietly, or pick my shoes off the floor. You're not like Gran, always telling me how much I've grown, and asking me what I'm going to do when I leave school. You don't want me different, like all my teachers do. You don't tease me, like Sue. And you don't run off and leave, like my dad.'

Tucking her under his arm, he gazed out over the water.

'I wouldn't mind you being real,' he said. 'Even if it was more work. Even if you howled, and kept filling your nappies, and threw giant tantrums in shops. I wouldn't mind.'

He peeped down at her, comfy and safe in his armpit, and pressed a finger where her nose would be, if she weren't just a bag of flour.

'I'll tell you what I don't understand,' he confided. 'I don't understand how people can treat babies badly.'

Her huge eyes stared up at him. He tried to explain.

'Mum says she knows how it happens.' Simon couldn't

help scowling. 'In fact, she says she wouldn't like to count the number of times I nearly copped it from her, when I was teething.'

He shook his head in amazement.

'And Gran says her sister lost her temper once, and threw her baby in the cot so hard that one of its legs broke.'

He bent his head closer.

'Not one of the baby's legs,' he explained. 'One of the cot's.'

Glad to have made that clear, he pressed on.

'And Sue claims she gets so ratty if she doesn't get a full eight hours uninterrupted sleep every night that it's a good thing she never had a family because, if she did, she'd murder all of them within a week.'

He pulled the flour baby on to his knee.

'And Mum went camping with Sue once, for only two nights, and came back saying she believed it.'

He poked her gently where her tummy would be.

'And look at Robin,' he said. 'He's usually easy-going enough. Puts up with Old Carthorse picking on him about keeping his rubber dropping collection in his desk, and puts up with all Wayne's jokes about him having two left feet. It's not like Robin to go totally ape like that.'

He stared over the flour baby's head, into the dark flowing water. It wasn't even, he thought, as if anything very special had happened to drive Robin wild. Certainly nothing to explain him seeing red like that, and getting in such a frenzy. All that had happened was that Gwyn had asked to borrow somebody's workbook.

'Why?'

'To copy out yesterday's homework.'

'You don't want mine, then,' Wayne had said. 'I got the whole lot wrong.'

'You don't want mine either,' George assured him. 'Carthorse told me a brain-dead troll could have made a better stab at it.'

To Gwyn, the actual quality of the work on offer was clearly a matter of total indifference.

'All Carthorse said was that I had to *do* it,' he explained. 'He didn't say anything about getting it *right*.'

'You can borrow mine if you like,' Robin offered. 'He never said it was rubbish so I think he must have liked it.'

'Right, then,' said Gwyn. 'I'll take yours.' And he stood by while Robin dug in his bag, pushing aside his maths textbook and the new French picture dictionary Mr Dupasque had insisted on giving him only that morning. In search of the homework, he dug too deeply too fast, and his flour baby fell out on the muddy path.

'Oh, shoot!'

Picking it up, he brushed the worst of the mud and gravel off, and tossed it to Gwyn for safekeeping.

True to form, Gywn dropped it.

It fell in the mud again. This time, Robin picked it up and stuck it firmly in a bush beside the path, before digging deeper in the bag. Above his own furious scrabblings, he didn't hear the soft ripping noise of the flour baby behind him. It was only when the little sacking bag had torn sufficiently to drop back in the mud with a soft floury splat that he even realized what was happening.

And that was the moment at which he lost his temper.

'Stupid!' he yelled. 'Stupid! Stupid! Stupid!'

Gwyn stepped back nervously. Was he being blamed? But no. It was the flour baby that had put Robin in a rage. Picking it off the ground, he'd shaken it till flour spilled.

'Stupid! Stupid!' he yelled again, punching it hard.

Flour puffed out in clouds.

Robin went berserk.

'Take care of your flour baby!' he screamed, in mimicry of all the adults who had been nagging him for days. 'Don't forget! Take it here! Take it there! Make sure you strap it safely on your bike! Don't lose it! Keep it out of the mud!'

For every order he shouted, he gave the flour baby a hard punch.

'Don't let it get wet! Don't dirty it! Make sure it doesn't fall! Don't forget to pretend it's a real baby!'

Now he was shaking it so fiercely the rip widened, and flour spilled on the path.

'Pretend you're real? Fine! I'll pretend you're real! And if you were real, if you were mine, I'd kick you in the canal!'

And then, before their very eyes, he'd drawn back his foot, let go of the flour sack, and done it.

Thwack!

Simon sat quietly on the bank, remembering how, just as the damaged sack had sunk at once, the flour along the path had blown away in an instant. In less than a minute there was nothing to see except a few sad, rising bubbles.

He hugged his own flour baby tightly to his chest.

'I don't know much,' he told her. 'But I do know this. I'd never do that to you. Never, never, never.'

And, at that moment, he believed himself.

Notes for Chapter 7

Back in Mr Cartright's classroom he reads from the diaries to keep the boys quiet. They are bored and badly behaved. Despite all this, it is clear from their diaries that they have learned something from looking after their flour babies. Even though he was pessimistic about the project in the beginning, Mr Cartright begins to feel happier with 4C.

What do you think?
What have Robin, Sajid, Wayne, Gwyn and Simon learned from the experience of the project?

Questions
1. Anne Fine uses humour in this chapter to interest the reader. Pick out two humorous moments of description, dialogue or action that you enjoyed reading.
2. Why does Mr Cartright give Simon the answer to the question about his father's song when he doesn't really know the answer?
3. Why do you think Mr Cartright is reasonably satisfied with his lesson in this chapter?

Further activity
In this chapter George tells the class that cooked babies taste exactly like pork. A famous eighteenth-century writer called Jonathan Swift wrote an article called 'A Modest Proposal' about this very topic. An extract from it is printed below. Find out the background to this article and why Swift wrote it. Like Anne Fine, he uses humour to address a serious topical issue:

I have been assured by a very knowing American of my acquaintance in London, that a young healthy child well nursed is at a year old a most delicious, nourishing, and wholesome food, whether stewed, roasted, baked, or boyled, and I make no doubt that it will equally serve in a fricasie, or a ragoust … Those who are more thrifty … may flay the carcass; the skin of which, artificially dressed, will make admirable gloves for ladies, and summer boots for fine gentlemen.

Chapter 7

On Day 16, Mr Cartright couldn't do a thing with them. Philip Brewster fell off his chair, arguing that the Chinese were the tallest people on earth. Luis Pereira kept pushing his desk out of line, over and over, till Mr Cartright realized Henry had convinced him that the spider on the ceiling just above his head was deadly poisonous, and also dribbling. Bill Simmons wouldn't stop adding rather unpleasant flourishes to the huge bluebottle tattoo he'd inked on his forearm. And even Robin Foster, who usually wasn't much trouble, kept flicking bits of his rubber dropping collection at the petunia on the window sill.

'Right!' said Mr Cartright. 'I know what we'll do. We'll have a few snippets from the diaries.'

He waited for the groaning to peak.

'Or –' he threatened. 'We could just have a second go at yesterday's disastrous test.'

Everyone settled down hastily to listen to the diaries. Gwyn Phillips laid his head gently on his flour baby, as though it were a pillow on the desk. His eyes closed, and his thumb crept in his mouth. Nobody scoffed. It was as if they took it for a signal that today was time out. It was back to the nursery.

Within moments, everyone had spread themselves as comfortably as possible. Some of them even copied Simon by propping their flour babies on the desk tops, as if they were listening too.

Mr Cartright began.

'I'll start with Henry,' he told them. 'Henry on Day 9.'

Henry's arm punched the air.

Mr Cartright began.

'"I hate my flour baby. I hate it worse than anything else on earth. It weighs about a ton. I asked my Dad how much I weighed when I was born, and he said he might have got me mixed up with our Jim or our Laura, but he thinks I weighed eight pounds. Eight pounds! That's another two on top of Fatso here! I asked Dad how much that was in kilos, and he went all snitty and said he cooked my supper and fixed my bike, I couldn't expect him to do my homework as well."'

Mr Cartright broke off.

A faint roar of approval came from those members of 4C who had both stayed awake and listened till the end.

'Now we'll have Tullis's,' said Mr Cartright. 'Since he's not here. This is Day 8. I should warn you Days 2 to 7 and 9 to 13 are unaccountably missing.'

He waited for the laughter to subside before reading out, with an expression of distaste:

'"My flour baby has a bogey down her front. I'm not flicking it off. It's not mine, so why should I?"'

He stopped.

'That's it.'

A cheer rose to greet this announcement.

Encouraged, Mr Cartright picked up Rick Tullis's effort for Day 14.

'"If I've been off a lot, you can blame the flour baby. I'm not saying I would have bothered to come much anyway. But what with that thing, I'm definitely staying away again tomorrow."'

Mr Cartright lifted his head to gaze round the class room.

'He's taken to numbering his sentences,' he informed them. 'In case he should make the terrible mistake of writing more than three.'

He rooted through the pile of diary entries.

'Here's something interesting,' he told them. 'Two exactly the same.'

He read the first aloud. It was by Wayne Driscoll.

'"*My mum says when I was born, we were so poor we practically lived in a bucket and ate coal. This was because my grandpa said I looked like a goblin. Mum stopped speaking to him, so he wouldn't lend her any money. Mum thinks he was fed up because I'm black and he isn't. Not that he's my dad, just my grandad, so what's it to him? I reckon my dad would have been a whole lot worse than fed up if I'd come out all white! Mum says she's no patience with either of them and wishes everyone in the world was green.*"'

Picking up another, scruffier, piece of paper, Mr Cartright read the whole sorry tale out over again, word for word.

One by one, they all raised their heads to look at Gwyn Phillips.

'What's the matter?' Gwyn demanded. 'Why are you all staring at me?'

'You can't just copy *anything*,' Robin Foster explained kindly. 'It has to make sense for *you*. And you're not *black*.'

Gwyn took to muttering. Very little was audible, except to his nearest neighbours. But some approximation to the phrase 'racial discrimination' could be heard coming up now and again in the course of his grumbling.

Mr Cartright ignored him.

'Shall we move on?' he asked pleasantly. 'Let's have Sajid Mahmoud on Day 14.'

Sajid stared round the room proudly, inviting admiration. A few of them took the trouble to scowl, but most pretended that they hadn't noticed him.

'"*By today, I should have made well over a hundred pounds, but what with six people not putting their flour babies in my crèche, and Tullis forever being off and me not thinking to start till Day 4, and some people not coughing up what they owe me in spite of having Henry and Luis set on them, I only have half of that so far. Still—*"'

Mr Cartright stopped on the upbeat, and waited for everyone to guess the end.

'*That's business*!' roared everyone, in unison.

Mr Cartright took time out to run his eyes over Sajid's work a second time.

'There's only two sentences here,' he warned.

Over and above Sajid's prolonged and furious disputation with Mr Cartright about the exact nature and role of the comma, some serious accusations could be heard from the others.

'… robbing us *blind*!'

'… chiselled me out of four weeks' pocket money already!'

'… *never* get round to paying for next door's coal bin at this rate …'

116

'Good as thieving, frankly…'

Mr Cartright shifted uncomfortably on the desk. Waving Sajid into silence, he reminded the others:

'Nobody forced you to put your flour babies in his crèche.'

Then, hastily, he picked up another sheet of paper.

'Here's Simon,' he told them. 'Simon on Day 12. "*I was really upset by Foster booting his flour baby in the canal like that. I never thought of Foster as a hard nugget before. In fact, he's a really good friend of mine. I expect that his problem is what Miss Arnott's always saying. He's rather immature.*"'

Mr Cartright raised his head from the paper in order to interrupt himself and say to Simon:

'I hope you realize that reading all this out so smoothly and evenly is a real triumph of the decipherer's art.'

Not really grasping the full force of Mr Cartright's insult, Simon contented himself with a sour grunt, which Mr Cartright chose to take as permission to carry on reading.

'"*My mum kept sticking up for Robin too. She said you can't go round giving people The Black Spot just because they do something daft, or I'd still be marked down for a bad lot for throwing that cactus at Hyacinth Spicer, or giving Tullis's alsatian my gran's wig to chew, and one or two other things I don't really want to write about in this diary.*"'

Unfortunately for Simon, George Spalder did not seem to share his very acute sense of privacy.

'I think he means the time he flushed his geography

117

project away, and flooded all the lavatories,' he confided to everyone.

'No,' said Tariq. 'He means the time he fed Miss Arnott's aspirins to the gerbil, and the poor thing fetched up in a coma.'

He looked round, to check no one had misunderstood.

'Not Miss Arnott,' he said, just in case doubt was lingering in anyone's mind. 'The gerbil.'

'No, no, no.' Impatiently, Wayne brushed Tariq's theory aside. 'He means the time he used that big red DANGER sign as a leg-up to get over the wire fence, and got caught leaning against that huge gas cylinder, having a quiet cigarette.'

By now, Mr Cartright was eyeing Simon with a new respect. A huge hunk of a lad, yes. And strong. But what he'd never realized before was what a swathe of mayhem the boy left behind, as he shambled through his life.

Then, suddenly noticing everyone looking at him expectantly, Mr Cartright felt obliged to come up with some suitably pedagogic response.

'You shouldn't smoke,' he scolded Simon. 'You might stunt your growth.'

And he went on to Philip Brewster, Day 10.

'"Bad times! I thought my flour baby was the pits, but next door have a real one and it's a yowler. On and on and on. I hear it through the wall. As I told Trish my goldfish, if it were mine, I'd tie its neck in a reef knot."'

Fascinated, Mr Cartright shuffled through the pages till

he found Philip Brewster, Day 11.

'"*What gets me is that I get seriously ticked off for playing my radio so soft I can't even* **hear** *it. This baby is switched up to Volume 10 all night, and when I come down in the morning firing on only one cylinder because I've had no sleep, everyone tells me we're lucky it isn't our baby. I wish it were. I'd soon put an end to its bleating.*"'

Everyone turned to look at Philip, who blushed.

'Go on,' Tariq begged Mr Cartright. 'Go on with the story, sir. Find his Day 12.'

Mr Cartright found Philip's Day 12.

'"*I went round and told that woman next door I wasn't getting much sleep, and she went totally unpicked. I only just managed to get off the doorstep ahead of the lava. I don't understand people with babies, really I don't.*"'

A warm, full-throated cheer of agreement greeted this last announcement.

'Yeh! People with babies have to be totally unhinged.'

'Barking mad.'

It was Sajid, as usual, who put the point over most coherently.

'I mean, they stroll round all day with these real ones tucked under their arms that keep bawling and messing and having to have their bums wiped –'

'Not just their bums!' interrupted Henry. 'My mum says you have to keep wiping their noses.'

'Grotesque!'

'Disgusting!'

'Just the thought of it makes you feel *sick*.'

119

'And then they yowl all night!'

A fresh onset of grumbling from the back row proved to be Philip Brewster's personal corroboration of this last complaint.

'That's all I said to her, that it had been yowling all night. And she went *unpicked*.'

Sajid went on with his allegations.

'And some of them are even heavier than ours. My aunty brings hers round and it weighs twenty-four pounds. Twenty-four pounds! And my aunty still has to carry it. It still can't walk!'

Wayne Driscoll broke in at this point. 'That's definitely the thing that gets me about them. They can't walk. They can't talk. They can't kick a ball, or even get the spoon anywhere near their own faces.'

'They're just a total nuisance.'

'You can't blame Robin for booting his in the canal.'

'His flour baby was *lucky*,' Tariq told them darkly. 'In the good old days, people used to dump babies out on the mountainside.'

'Or cook and eat them.'

Mr Cartright felt obliged to step in at this point to pull 4C's lively discussion back on the rails.

'No, I don't think so, George. Not cook and eat them.'

'Oh yes, sir.' George was adamant. 'They taste exactly like pork. I read it in a book.'

The general clamour for more information was almost

drowned out by potential individual researchers.

'What book?'

'Do you still have it?'

'Can I borrow it?'

'*Pork*?'

'What about crackling? Do babies make proper crackling?'

Hastily, Mr Cartright wellied in again.

'People with babies aren't all barking mad,' he told them. 'In fact, any one of you lot might choose to have one some day. Not to mention the fact that many people fetch up with babies by accident.'

The rush of feeling engendered by this observation astonished even Mr Cartright.

'That's terrible, that is!'

'Having a baby by accident!'

'Strick!'

'I'd *never* have one by accident. Never!'

Bill Simmons seemed almost in tears at the idea.

'It's horrible even to think about. One careless moment and then – hell on wheels!'

Gwyn clearly agreed with him.

'Your whole life ruined by *one slip*.'

'Shocking!'

Luis Pereira took full advantage of his reputation for knowing more girls than anyone else in the class.

'And it might not even be your fault,' he warned them all conspiratorially.

There was sheer consternation at the thought that

anyone present might end up with a baby through no real fault of his own. For the second time in under three weeks, 4C fell absolutely silent.

Russ Mould rose to his feet.

'Suppose –'

Words failed him.

Mr Cartright looked at him encouragingly.

'Yes, lad?'

'Suppose –'

Once again, Russ couldn't carry on.

Mr Cartright looked blank. But all the others were clearly finding it easier to interpret the look of baffled horror on Russ's face.

'Yes! Yes! Russ is right! Suppose you get stuck –'

'*With* someone –'

'And you're not absolutely sure –'

'Might not be safe.'

'You can always say no,' Wayne Driscoll responded virtuously.

The others seemed satisfied with this.

'That's right.'

'Just say no.'

'Not worth taking any risks,' Phil Brewster told them all sagely.

'Better be safe than sorry.'

'One sloppy moment, and your life's not your own.'

Mr Cartright gazed out at the worried faces, all struggling with the idea of having to defend themselves against the terrible dangers on the horizon. Only one member of the class didn't seem swept up in the general anxiety, and that was Simon Martin. Simon was sitting chewing his pen, and staring thoughtfully out of the window. He'd been quiet throughout the whole hubbub. Mr Cartright was pretty sure he understood why Simon hadn't joined in the general pillorying of the flour babies. After all, he'd taken such a strong shine to his own that his psychology had been a matter of heated discussion for over two weeks now in the staffroom, with half the teachers insisting the poor boy was in dire need of professional counselling, and the rest lining up behind Mr Dupasque and Miss Arnott to claim his response was 'rather sweet', and more to be applauded than pitied.

But what was he thinking now? What was on his mind?

Deliberately, Mr Cartright picked out the semiliterate Russ Mould to read the names on top of the diary entries and distribute them back to their owners. Then, under the cover of the spreading riot, he slid off his desk and made his way round the class till he was beside Simon and could ask him privately:

'A penny for your thoughts?'

Simon glanced up.

'I was just thinking about my father,' he said.

Mr Cartright gave this response a moment's consideration. You had to be careful. These days, some parents swapped spouses round like first day cover stamps, or football cards. Only the week before, he'd strolled behind a couple of pupils working side by side, and heard one saying to the other, amiably enough: 'You've got my old dad now, haven't you?' No, you had to be very much on your guard.

'Do you have a new one I don't yet know about?' he asked Simon politely.

'No,' Simon said. 'I was thinking about my real one. I can't help wondering about him. He's on my mind.'

Mr Cartright trod as carefully as he could.

'Is there anything in particular bothering you?'

'Yes. Yes, there is,' said Simon. 'There's something I really want to know.'

Mr Cartright pitched his voice over the growing tumult behind them.

'What?'

'What he was whistling.'

Mr Cartright was mystified.

'What he was whistling?'

'When he left,' Simon explained. 'I want to know what he was whistling the day he walked out.'

Mr Cartright was floored. After a moment, he patted Simon affectionately on the shoulder.

'Sorry, lad,' he said gently. 'Not on the syllabus.'

He was on the verge of adding, under his breath:

'Nothing of much use is,' when suddenly it struck him he didn't mean it and it wasn't true. They'd learned a lot from this Science Fair project, for example. Dr Feltham was right. They'd learned about the tedium of responsibility, its endless grind, and how they felt about it. Mild little Robin Foster had even learned he had a serious temper. Sajid had learned (if he didn't know already) he had a healthy entrepreneurial streak. And every single one of them now knew that, old enough to father a baby as he might be, he was not yet old enough to be a father.

Every single one of them?

Maybe not. Mr Cartright still had his doubts about Simon. There the lad sat, his huge limbs folded uncomfortably under his desk, fingering the grey lace on his flour baby's bonnet and sunk morosely in thought.

Was he still wondering about his father? Or was he, as half the staffroom insisted, going broody with longing for a real baby of his own?

Either way, it was time to put a stop to it. Mr Cartright had never claimed to be a patient man. And it was at this moment that he decided that he'd had enough. There was, after all, almost a whole year of teaching the boy still ahead. He couldn't stand this woebegone face, these glum looks. Up until now, Mr Cartright had not really noticed that many compensations came his way for having to teach 4C. But now he saw that most of them, even if they weren't all that bright, did at least make the effort to stay chirpy. Wasn't there some old sea song about being of good cheer?

Kill two birds with one stone, thought Mr Cartright.

Reaching down, he snatched Simon's flour baby off the desk, and put it behind his back, where Simon couldn't see it. Only when he was sure he had the boy's full attention did he say:

'I'll tell you what your dad was whistling.'

The tone of utter confidence with which Mr Cartright made this pronouncement caused Simon's eyes to widen.

'When he walked out, your dad was whistling "Sail Away",' Mr Cartright told the boy with utter finality. 'That's what he was whistling: "Sail Away".'

He didn't hang around for Simon to start asking how he knew, or ask him to hum the melody or remember the words. He simply dropped Simon's flour baby back on the desk, and took off as fast as a man of his bulk could go, across the room, not even slowing up to pull the occasional pair of pugilists apart, or tell Luis to stop chipping at his desk top.

He didn't stop until he reached his desk.

'Right!' he bellowed. 'That's it. I've had enough. It's nearly time, so clear off, the whole lot of you. Go home.'

This precipitated the usual tiresome performance, but in reverse this time.

'But, sir! Sir! The bell hasn't rung yet!'

'Just go, Tariq. Go home, all of you, before I change my mind.'

He sat watching the usual riot and confusion that took place as they poured out. Simon wasn't the first to reach the door, he noticed; but neither was he by any means the last. And the troubled look on his face had vanished. The power was back in his stride.

Content, Mr Cartright started to pack his own briefcase,

ready to take off home. Not a bad lesson for 4C, he thought. Not bad. Not bad.

Contrary to expectation – against all odds – he'd managed to do something with them.

Notes for Chapter 8

Simon begins to understand the reasons for his father's behaviour and finds out the words to the song he might have been singing when he left. Notice how strands of the novel begin to link together to form the whole. You can begin to identify some of the problems and issues that have run through the novel, and develop later to give us a satisfying ending.

What do you think?
Previous tensions are being resolved. Think about:
- how Mr Cartright and Simon become closer
- how Simon Martin and Martin Simon become linked, despite their differences at the beginning of the novel.

Questions
1. What device does Anne Fine use to make you want to read on at the end of the section with Hyacinth Spicer?
2. 'The pause that followed lasted a beat too long. It was, Mr Cartright thought, a bit like that old oriental torture of waiting for the water drip.' (page 140). Why is Mr Cartright in such suspense? Read the paragraph before it, to help you with your answer.
3. Can you explain the reason why Simon's father left? Can you see how the metaphor from the song helps explain his actions?

Further activities
1. Write Simon's flour baby diary entry for today. You might like to think about the following:
   - how he feels about his mother
   - how he feels about Hyacinth Spicer and 'ear'oles' who work hard at school
   - how he feels about his flour baby
   - how he feels about his father.

2. 'Maybe the reason why his father left was that ... he wasn't up to the job.' Write a formal advert for an ideal father. Think carefully about the serious qualities that are needed, as well as the kind of interests and personality he might need.

Chapter 8

'Go on,' said Simon. 'Sing it.'

'I can't.' Simon's mother turned to catch Macpherson creeping up on the flour baby, and swatted him with the tea towel. 'You know I can't sing.'

'I'm not planning to give you marks out of ten,' Simon assured her. 'I just want to hear the words, and learn the tune.'

'I don't know all the words. I'm not even sure I'd get the tune right.'

'Go on,' Simon insisted. 'Have a go.'

So Mrs Martin had a go. Wiping her hands dry, she leaned back against the sink, and, while Simon rocked the flour baby in his arms, deliberately provoking Macpherson into yelping spasms of jealousy, she sang out as bravely as she could.

'Unfurl the sail, lads, and let the winds find me
Breasting the soft, sunny, blue rising main –'

She broke off.

Simon looked up.

'Well?' he demanded. 'What's the problem?'

'I've forgotten the next bit.'

Simon sighed with exasperation.

'But that was only *two lines*. You only sang *two lines*.'

Mrs Martin threw the tea towel at Macpherson, who was surreptitiously taking advantage of the lull in the rocking to chew a bit more off one of the flour baby's corners.

'Two lines is all I can remember.'

'Pathetic,' said Simon.

He looked so morose, Mrs Martin felt sorry for him.

'Maybe the rest will come back to me,' she tried to console him.

But Simon wasn't in the mood for waiting.

'I know,' he said. 'We'll ring Sue.'

Dumping the flour baby on the seat of the chair, he made for the telephone.

Shaking her head, Mrs Martin asked her son:

'And why should Sue know the words?'

He didn't dare suggest that, if it was the song his father had been whistling the very last time Sue ever saw him, then she might very well have tucked little snatches of it away in her brain.

He thrust the phone at his mother.

'Just ring and ask.'

'Don't be silly, Simon,' said Mrs Martin.

She reached down to prise the flour baby out from between Macpherson's teeth as, seizing his chance, he tried to slink past her to the door. 'I can't just ring Sue to ask her to sing down the phone.'

'Why not?'

Put to the test, Mrs Martin couldn't think of any reason. So while Simon used a clean pair of underpants from the laundry pile to try to wipe the worst of Macpherson's slobber off the flour baby, she made the call.

And Sue, when she answered, didn't seem to find the request at all strange. Even before Simon could snatch the phone from his mother's ear, and put it to his own, he could hear her chirruping away down the line.

'Toss all my burdens and woes clear behind me,

Vow I'll not carry those cargoes again.'

Then, just like his mother, Sue broke off.

'I've forgotten the chorus,' she told him. 'Something about sunrise, and being of good cheer.'

It was only the warning look on his mother's face that turned Simon's howl of frustration into a meagre grunt of thanks. Handing the phone back, he banged his fist against the kitchen door in sheer irritation, and then, when it flew open, felt obliged to walk through, because his mother was still watching him.

In the shared yard, Hyacinth Spicer was sitting daintily on an upturned bucket, dyeing her sandals green. Hyacinth probably knew the whole song, Simon thought moodily. Learned it at Brownies, brushed it up at Little Woodland Folk, and sang the descant in the Baptist church choir. But he'd be happily boiled in oil before he'd ask Hyacinth Spicer any favours. He already suspected her of being one of Mr Cartright's spies: a good amateur turned professional. He was on the verge of turning back into the house when Hyacinth herself raised the topic spontaneously.

'Was that your mum singing?' she asked. Then, dabbing dye carefully on her sandal strap. 'Not very good, is she?'

An idea struck Simon. Worth a try, anyway.

'It's a very hard song to sing,' he said.

Hyacinth looked up in surprise.

'No, it isn't.'

'Of course it is,' Simon insisted. 'The chorus is particularly tricky.'

'No, it isn't.'

And, her capacity for showing off undimmed since the day Miss Ness first pinned the huge tinfoil star of Bethlehem to her woolly in nursery school, Hyacinth threw back her head and sang:

'Sail for a sunrise that burns with new maybes,

Farewell, my loved ones, and be of good cheer.

Others may settle to dandle their babies –'

Just at that moment, she glanced down and noticed the dye dripping into her sandal.

'Oh, sh – ugar!'

Simon tried tempting her into singing what he could tell, from the sheer swell of the melody, must be the one, last, elusive line.

'I expect you dripped that deliberately,' he said. 'Since it's the end of the song that's the hardest to sing well.'

But Hyacinth Spicer had completely lost interest. She was intent on mopping up her shoe.

'Shove off, Simon,' she told him, just softly enough for both of them to be able to pretend he hadn't heard.

Simon went back inside. Shutting the door carefully, so Hyacinth Spicer couldn't hear, he sang what he'd learned of the chorus to his mother. But though she claimed then, and several times later that evening, that the last line was on the tip of her tongue, she never managed to come out with it.

By morning, Simon was in the sort of mental state he associated with victims of the water-drip torture.

'I'm going mad,' he told his mother over breakfast. 'It's driving me insane.'

'You could go and be nice to Hyacinth. She'd sing you the last line.'

The scowl Simon turned on her was prodigious.

Mrs Martin shrugged.

'Then you'll just have to ask Mr Cartright.'

Ask Mr Cartright! Simon shovelled more cereal in his mouth, and used the freshly-licked spoon to poke the flour baby.

'This is your fault,' he told her. And it was. If it weren't for her, he realized, he would never have started to take an interest in his father, and what happened years ago. Without this stupid, useless, floppy bag of flour, he'd never have ended up in the awful, shaming position he was in today – keen to get off to school to learn something, like a proper ear'ole.

He prodded the flour baby again. This time, a few drips of muddy brown milk from his bran cereal slid off his spoon and slithered down her front.

'You'll catch it,' his mother warned him cheerily. 'Look at the poor little mite. Slobber, toothmarks, bran-smears. And that's just the last five minutes.'

'She's all right,' Simon said shortly. He poked her again. 'Aren't you?'

The flour baby didn't demur. But peering more closely as he shoved her away in his bag, Simon could see that she was hardly in a state to pass muster at the twice-weekly weigh-in. Not only had she become grimy beyond belief over the last few days, but her corners were frayed and her bottom was leaking.

Simon gave her the look that never failed to send Miss Arnott scurrying for her aspirins. How could something that couldn't even walk get into such a mess? What a hiccup!

And now his mother was handing him a plastic bag.

'You'd better take this for her,' she warned. 'The forecast is rain.'

He could have pointed out that any rainwater that fell on the flour baby might clean her up a bit, or make up some weight from the leakage. But, frankly, he couldn't be bothered. He was sick of the whole business.

Forcing the last spoonfuls of bran into his already bulging cheeks, he made a noise he hoped his mother would be charitable enough to take for a goodbye, and scooped up his school things and his flour baby.

Mrs Martin stood firmly between him and the door.

'Goodbye, Simon,' she said pointedly.

His mouth still stuffed to bursting, he grunted again.

She stood her ground.

'Goodbye, Simon,' she repeated patiently.

He recognized it for the yellow card.

He stood there, like a huge dummy, making the effort to chew and swallow his huge mouthful of bran.

Then:

'Bye, Mum.'

She smiled at last, letting him off the hook. He took off down the path, leaving the door swinging on its hinges. Strange, he was thinking, how parents, like teachers, could keep up the nagging for years and years about tin-pot things like saying thank you and goodbye. He didn't know how they did it. He'd go unhinged within a week. Every single morning he went through this performance with his mother about emptying his mouth and saying goodbye properly. Every single school morning! That was five times a week, thirteen weeks a term, three terms a year. Every year. How many times was that? Millions, at least. So how did she manage to stand there each day and go through the whole thing without flying off the handle and going at him with a meat-axe? He certainly wouldn't manage it, that was for sure. He thought of himself as patient as the next man. But if he had to remind the flour baby more than a dozen times in a row about not leaving the back door wide open, or turning off the hot tap properly, or talking with her mouth full, he'd do a Foster and boot her straight in the canal. Maybe the reason why his father left was that, like Simon, he realized almost straight away he wasn't up to the job.

Reaching the end of Wilberforce Road, Simon unaccountably burst into song.

'*Others may settle to dandle their babies –*' he warbled lustily, as, rounding the corner, he tripped over Wayne Driscoll who was fiddling about in the gutter.

'What are you doing in that drain?' Simon asked, picking himself up, and loath to believe the evidence of his own eyes, since Wayne appeared to be stooped over the grating, scooping up dirt and trickling it between his fingers into his flour baby through a small tear in the fabric.

Wayne's brows were knitted in the fiercest concentration.

'Hold it steady for me, Sime. I can't get this dirt down the little hole.'

Simon squatted in the gutter and took Wayne's bag of flour from him.

'You could make the hole bigger,' he suggested.

Wayne snorted.

'Oh, ace idea, Sime! Give Old Carthorse *two* reasons to maul me!'

With his free hand, Simon tipped his own flour baby out of his bag.

'If you're in trouble, so am I,' he said. 'Mine looks a lot worse than yours.'

Wayne took a break from trickling dirt to glance at Simon's flour baby.

'Strick, Sime! What a grime-bag! You'll catch it this morning.'

'No, I won't,' Simon said confidently. Then, slightly less sure, he took another look. Maybe he would. No doubt about it, his flour baby was a mess. How had it happened? How did she get so mucky so quickly? One moment Simon was Star of the Project, with teachers he barely knew nodding affectionately at him in the corridors. The next, he was carrying about a manky leaking sack of flour with two smudged eyes and chewed corners. What went wrong?

'You should never have let Hooper and Phillips use her as a goal marker,' Wayne was telling him.

Simon defended himself as best he could.

'That didn't make much difference. What got her so torn was using her to tease Hyacinth Spicer's cat.'

'I don't think that the rips look nearly as bad as the chewed bits,' Wayne observed dispassionately.

'I blame Macpherson,' Simon said gloomily. 'He's had it in for my flour baby since the very first day.'

'What about those black smudges?'

'Fell in the grate, didn't she?'

'And the nasty charred bits?'

'Oh, those are my fault,' Simon admitted. 'I left her on the grill while I made toast.'

'What about all this stuff stuck to her bum?'

Simon upturned her, and inspected her.

'Glue,' he said. 'Lump of toffee. Mud. Macpherson's dried dribble. Chicken korma soup –'

There was enough to keep the litany up for quite a while. But, hastily, Wayne interrupted him.

'Come on, Sime. Time to go.'

And confident that, at the very least, he wouldn't come off worst at the morning inspection, Wayne pulled Simon with him along the road. As they reached the roundabout, Simon took to explaining the problem he had with the flour baby.

'I'm not the type, you see. I thought I was, at first. But it turned out that I was wrong. Some people are good at looking after things. Some people aren't. I reckon I'm out of the second box. More like my dad.'

Wayne shot him a curious look, making Simon realize it must be the very first time his friend had ever heard him bring up the subject of his father. But he pressed on anyway.

'He couldn't handle it either, that's obvious. Maybe some people can't. Maybe they're just like that, and you can't blame them.'

As usual, he stepped out fearlessly into the stream of cars slowing unwillingly for the roundabout.

'He just wasn't the sort to settle and dandle his babies,' he yelled, over the roar of the traffic.

As usual, Wayne scurried in his wake, nodding apologetically to all the drivers Simon had just brought screeching to a halt.

'Wasn't the sort to *what*?'

But Simon was over the road now, and striding purposefully across the grass towards the school buildings. There was one last thing he wanted to find out, one last clue to the mystery of his father's disappearance. One thing he still needed to know.

'Miss Arnott! Miss Arnott!'

She turned as soon as she heard him.

'What is it, Simon?'

To her astonishment, he started to sing at her in the rich, robust, unembarrassed tenor voice she'd heard often enough in Assembly, and never realized belonged to him.

'*Unfurl the sail, lads, and let the winds find me –*'

'Simon?'

'*Breasting the soft, sunny, blue rising main –*'

Was he giving her a bit of cheek?

'I'm in a hurry, Simon,' she told him, as a warning. But he kept pace with her along the path, still singing heartily.

'*Toss all my burdens and woes clear behind me –*'

'Is this a joke, Simon? A bet? A sponsored sing?'

'*Vow I'll not carry those cargoes again.*'

Impatient, she turned away, along the narrower path that led to the staff door. Totally ignoring the strict school rule, and the sign on the little wooden post: *Staff only beyond this point*, Simon charged along beside her, still singing his powerful heart out.

'*Sail for a sunrise that burns with new maybes,*
Farewell, my loved ones –'

Miss Arnott stopped in her tracks. She'd never faced this problem with Simon before. Moody and awkward he could be. And downright troublesome on some occasions. But she had to admit that, in all her experience of the boy, she'd never known him truly disobedient. What should she do? Tackle him? Or ignore it? First things first, thought Miss Arnott. Who was watching?

She glanced up to where, framed in the staffroom window, Mr Cartright was blowing the smoke of his last surreptitious cigarette before class, out between the folds of the curtain.

He gave a little wave, then, taking her look of temporary indecision for one of pitiful entreaty, he threw up the sash window, all set to bellow at Simon for daring to set foot on hallowed turf.

' – *and be of good cheer,*' he heard Simon singing at the top of his voice.

Be of good cheer? The snatch of song rang a bell instantly in Mr Cartright's brain. He couldn't help staring down at Simon with a teacherly blend of pleasure and pride. What price psychology now? Why, the lad was a walking tribute to good old-fashioned horse sense. Look at the change in him, for heaven's sake. One morning he was moping around like a fool, in love with his revolting little sack of flour. A word in his ear from his wise old class teacher, and look at him. Right back to normal (well, normal for *him,* of course), and courting the only real love of his life, the heavenly Miss Arnott, in fine voice, and full throttle.

'*Others may settle to dandle their babies –*' Simon's glorious warm tenor rang out, over the grounds.

The pause that followed lasted a beat too long. It was, Mr Cartright thought, a bit like that old oriental torture of waiting for the water drip.

When he could stand it no longer, he threw the window up higher, leaned out and roared in the great, tuneful baritone he used to haul them back to time in hymns:

'*My heart's a tall ship, and high winds are near.*'

Simon dropped to his knees, exhausted. Miss Arnott fled. And Wayne came thumping up behind.

'What was Old Carthorse bellowing about?'

'*My heart's a tall ship,*' panted Simon. '*And high winds are near.*'

Wayne made a face.

'What's that supposed to mean?'

Simon looked up to ask Mr Cartright. But it was too late. Perfectly content with the satisfactory rounding off of a lovely old sea song, Mr Cartright had stubbed out his cigarette, pulled down the window, and vanished.

As had been proved more than once on the football field, dogged determination was one of Wayne's most salient characteristics.

'How can a heart be a tall ship?' he persisted.

'I don't know, do I?' snapped Simon. 'We'll have to ask someone.'

'Who?'

Wayne looked round. The only person in sight was Martin Simon, who was strolling along the path reading *The Quest for the Holy Grail*.

'Ask him. He's an ear'ole. He might know.'

Simon's face brightened. Yes, Martin Simon might know. Anyone who puffed round all day reading poetry – often in French – was bound to have no trouble putting a fancy line of a song into plain English. No trouble at all.

Simon picked himself off his knees, and walked over the grass, till he was almost directly in front of Martin. Sticking out his foot, he waited calmly and deliberately until Martin tripped over it, and *The Quest for The Holy Grail* fell out of his hand on to the grass.

'Sorry,' said Simon, stooping to pick it up and hand it back.

'Thanks,' Martin said, somewhat warily.

But Simon felt that, by reaching down to pick up the book, he had already established his good faith. There was no need for any further tact.

'Look,' he said. 'You're an ear'ole. You read poetry. What does it mean if someone says they're a tall ship?'

Martin hesitated. It could be the start of a tease. But, on the other hand, there was a serious and determined look about Simon, as if, like Sir Galahad in the book that he'd just handed back, he was on some sort of quest.

'A tall ship?'

'Yes, a tall ship.'

You had to hand it to these clever dicks, Simon reflected as he stood waiting for the answer. If anyone strolled up to him and asked him a question like that, he'd push them in the face and stride off. But Martin didn't seem to find it either odd or insulting to be asked a question about what might even be a poem. He simply took off his glasses and wiped them while he had a little think, then asked:

'What did this person say *exactly*?'

No point in beating round the bush, thought Simon. So, throwing back his head, he sang out full-throatedly:

'*Others may settle to dandle their babies,*

My heart's a tall ship, and high winds are near.'

Martin's look of confusion cleared instantly. 'Well, obviously it's a metaphor,' he began. 'The protagonist has chosen to use the analogy of –'

He stopped, partly from terror, and partly because Simon's sudden grip on his throat had cut off the air in his windpipe.

'I wasn't asking for a *lecture*,' Simon informed him sternly. 'I just want to know what it *means*.'

He took his hand away, and stood waiting.

Martin Simon tried again.

'What it *means*,' he said. 'Is that the fellow has to go. Just as a ship with its sails spread has to move with the winds, so this chap knows the moment is coming when, however much he may *want* to stay, the sort of person he is – the sort of character and temperament he has – is going to force him to leave. He has no choice.'

Simon stared up at the sky. His eyes were prickling, and he swallowed hard.

'No choice?'

Martin said firmly:

'None at all. That's just the way it is with someone like him.'

At this point, Wayne broke in, asking Martin suspiciously:

'How can you be so sure?'

'It's in the *words*,' Martin explained patiently. 'That's what they *mean*.'

'But how do you *know*?'

It was Simon who came to Martin's rescue, putting Wayne firmly in his place.

'Listen,' he said. 'You and me, we know how to play football and have a good laugh, right? Now Martin here, he's an ear'ole. He's useless at football. He couldn't kick a jelly in a drain. But he knows about things like songs and poetry.'

He turned to Martin.

'Isn't that right?'

Martin nodded.

'Right,' Simon said. And then, since the discussion of cultural strengths and weaknesses seemed to have petered to a halt:

'Well, thanks very much.'

On an impulse, he stuck out his right arm. For just a moment Martin couldn't fathom why, and then he realized Simon wanted to shake hands with him.

'That's all right,' he said, responding as promptly as he could. 'Any time.'

'No,' Simon assured him. 'That's it, I expect. I'm pretty sure I'll be all right now.'

And indeed, Martin couldn't help thinking, there was a strange, unearthly look about him once again, almost an aura, as if, like Sir Galahad, he'd seen his vision of the Holy Grail, and knew he'd come across his heart's desire.

Chapter 6

Notes for Chapter 9

The Glorious Explosion could never happen in reality. But in this chapter Anne Fine gives us a few smaller explosions: Mr Cartright's laughter when he finds out about the expected Glorious Explosion and a light fitting breaking into smithereens. In Mr Cartright's classroom it is the end of the flour babies' project and diaries are being finished off. Mr Cartright begins to feel more sympathy for Simon as he understands more about his home life and his character, rather than just judging him on appearances and his poor performance in the classroom.

What do you think?
In this chapter Anne Fine involves us particularly with the characters of Mr Cartright and Simon. Has your opinion of the teacher changed at all during the novel? Why do you feel sympathy for Simon as you read on?

Questions
Look for sections in the text that support your answers to these questions:
1. Why does Simon act submissively to Mr Cartright and drop the oscilloscopes and follow him down the corridor?
2. What are the reasons for Mr Cartright collecting in the flour babies four days early?
3. There are many reasons why Simon is crying. Think of three factors.
4. Look at the way Anne Fine describes Mr Cartright's laugh. What does 'seismically' mean? Trace the words she uses to build up her description to show this.

Further activity
'But it's *disgusting*,' he thundered. 'It's utterly revolting. It's in the most disgraceful state. It's an absolute *outrage*.' (page 156).

Write a formal letter to Mr Cartright from Simon, outlining his excuse for the state of his flour baby. Make sure your language is persuasive enough to keep out of detention. You might like to look in Chapter 8 (pages 136–137) for some reasons for its dirty condition.

Chapter 9

Miss Arnott rooted in her bag for aspirins.

'That's the third time he's tramped past this door, singing at the top of his voice.' She turned to Mr Spencer, who was hunched over the staffroom table, rubbing the pencilled black centres out of most of the crotchets in the song books to try and turn them back into minims. 'Why can't you teach them quieter songs?'

Without raising his eyes from his salvage work, Mr Spencer defended himself calmly.

'I never taught him that one. And what you teach them makes no difference. Those lads in 4C would belt out a cradle song as if it were a battle hymn. There's nothing I can do about it. Just thank your lucky stars the boy has a fine voice.'

Miss Arnott dropped a second aspirin in her water glass.

'Call it a staff rest period,' she muttered bitterly. 'It's just a different way of suffering.'

She lifted her head.

'Is that him coming back again? I can't *bear* it. What is the boy doing, traipsing up and down this corridor, time and again?'

Mr Henderson broke off sipping coffee to tell her.

'If it's Simon Martin you're complaining about,' he said, 'Dr Feltham roped him in to carry Nimmo-Smith's Microprocessor Controlled Pedestrian Crossing along to its stand for the Science Fair. For once, the boy's only doing what he's told.'

'Was he told to sing sea shanties at full tilt while he did it?'

'Shall I tell him to turn down the volume?' Mr Henderson stuck his head round the staffroom door, but he was a moment too late. Mr Cartright had already appeared at the other end of the corridor.

'Simon Martin!' he bellowed, cutting the enthusiastic tenor off at source. 'Why aren't you down here at our weigh-in?'

Simon stopped short with his arms full of oscilloscope.

'I'm carrying stuff for Dr Feltham, sir,' he answered in the virtuous tones of one who knows himself to be girded with the strength of a more powerful teacher. 'It's for the Science Fair.'

Mr Cartright's face darkened. Science Fair! Science Fair! There was still half a week before it even started, and already he was heartily sick of it. Why, the business disrupted the whole term. If every other school in creation could tack this sort of licensed chaos on to the very last week, why on earth couldn't Dr Feltham? Really, the man was getting too big for his boots.

Mutiny rose in Mr Cartright. Before he could stop himself, a string of unteacherly words sprang from his lips and rang down the corridor with such force that Simon was shocked. Not that he hadn't used language as bad as that himself. Worse, in fact. And quite often. But for Old Carthorse to start frothing at the mouth, and let fly with such a blue flood – well!

Simon gazed at his teacher with a new respect.

'And as for you!' Mr Cartright finished up, glowering horribly at Simon. 'You can just put down that pile of junk, and come back to the classroom for the weigh-in.'

'Yes, sir.'

Simon laid the oscilloscopes and Wishart's Digital Sine Wave Generator down on the floor, and submissively fell in behind as his teacher strode off down the corridor.

'That's better,' muttered Mr Cartright. All very well, he was thinking, this business of Simon being of good cheer. But unfortunately, just like anything else in a school, it could be taken just that bit too far.

His bad mood lasted as far as the classroom.

'Right!' he bellowed, as he came through the door in time to catch Philip Brewster practising scissor jumps over Sajid's prams. 'That's it! I've had enough! You can just push that tin juggernaut in the corner, and line up with your little sacks of flour. I'm taking them in, and giving them back to Dr Feltham.'

'Giving them *back*?'

Mr Cartright totally misunderstood the nature of their astonishment and concern.

'Yes. Giving them back. I know it's four days too early, but you can just spend the time getting your diaries up to date.'

'But –'

'No buts!' roared Mr Cartright. 'Just get your flour babies, please, everyone.'

He stood beside the scales.

'Who wants to be first?'

From the thunderstruck silence that followed, he took it that no one wanted to be first.

'How about you, George?'

George was too baffled even to shake his head.

'Henry?'

Henry looked to the others to sort out this obvious oversight. But, seeing him turn away, Mr Cartright moved on impatiently.

'What about Rick? Not here? No, of course not. What about you, then, Russ? Are you ready to hand over your flour sack? One last weighing, and the thing will be off your hands for ever. How does that sound?'

Russ glanced up from picking cat hairs off his flour baby. He didn't realize that, by now, everyone else in the class was staring at Simon Martin expectantly, waiting for the one amongst them who had first burst in extolling the virtues of this particular experiment to break out of his ashen-faced paralysis and clear up this obvious confusion about the way it should end. Returning his attention to picking off the cat hairs, Russ simply asked:

'But what about the Glorious Explosion?'

Mr Cartright stared.

'The Glorious *What*?'

'The Glorious Explosion.' Russ looked up again. 'Simon told us that, on the last day, there'd be a Glorious Explosion. We'd all get to kick our flour babies to bits.'

'Kick them to bits?'

Mr Cartright could scarcely hide his amusement. 'Kick the flour babies to bits? And you believed him?'

He looked round and saw all their crestfallen expressions.

'You did!' he declared. 'You all believed him!'

He turned to Simon, whose stupefaction was giving way to deep embarrassment.

'You managed to convince them that, on the last day, they'd get to kick over a hundred pounds of sifted white flour around?'

Simon nodded.

Mr Cartright spread his arms wide.

'Here? In my classroom?'

Simon nodded again.

And then, slowly, seismically, Mr Cartright began chuckling. As he gripped the sides of his desk to steady himself, the chuckling grew. It grew from chuckles into loud guffaws, and from guffaws into huge rocking laughter. From huge rocking laughter it became an earthquake of merriment. Tears of amusement flooded from his eyes. The desk beneath him pitched and rolled. The windows rattled in their frames, and, next door, Miss Arnott feared for her wall display.

Mr Cartright pointed at Simon.

'You – You –'

For quite a while, he couldn't get it out.

'You told them they would be allowed to kick one hundred pounds of sifted white flour around in my classroom!'

He fished in his jacket pocket and drew out his huge spotted handkerchief. He wiped his streaming eyes.

'And they believed you!'

Still laughing fit to bust, he fell off his desk and landed on the floor. The boards shook. The desk careered over backwards, snapping the steel-tipped wooden blackboard rule in two, trapping one half beneath, and sending the other flying up at the ceiling where it hit the central light fitting.

BANG!!!!!!

There was a glorious explosion. Showers of sparks and splintered glass rained down on them, and their gasps of astonishment and delight were drowned by the hissing and spitting of ancient and overstressed electrical wiring.

The silence that followed was palpable. Then,

'See?' Robin said loyally. 'Simon was right.'

Loyally, too, he went off with his friend, to fetch the broom and the dustpan. Together they swept the shards of glass into a neat pile behind the door, and set Mr Cartright's desk back on its legs.

Mr Cartright set the scales down.

'Right,' he said. 'Joke over.'

He pointed at Russ, as the nearest.

'Hand over your flour baby.'

Not knowing what else to do, Russ passed his flour baby to Mr Cartright, who dumped it on the scale.

'Not bad, Russ. It's only lost a tiny bit of weight, and, apart from the cat hairs, it looks almost presentable. Well done!'

152

Mr Cartright dropped the flour baby into the huge double-duty black bin bag he'd been keeping in his desk for the occasion.

'One!' he said, cheering visibly.

He pointed again.

'Gwyn.'

Gwyn glanced at Sajid who, shrugging, reached in the pram crèche to pull out Gwyn's little sack of flour.

'We'll settle up now, shall we?' Sajid asked sweetly, deliberately holding Gwyn's flour baby over the muddy upturned spikes of Philip Brewster's running shoes.

Business was business, after all.

Scowling, Gwyn dipped his hands deep in his pockets and pulled out enough cash to redeem his flour baby.

'There you are,' he said sourly, handing it to Mr Cartright.

Mr Cartright dumped the flour bag unceremoniously on his scales.

'Lovely,' he said. 'Spot on!' And tossed it merrily into the bin bag.

'Next?'

Before it was too late, Sajid decided to seize the chance to force public payment on some of his most persistent defaulters. He reached in the pram crèche, and dug out Luis Pereira's flour baby. Accepting defeat as graciously as he could, Luis paid up, and took the flour sack to Mr Cartright, who weighed it.

'This one's gained a bit of weight,' he said. And then he noticed the sandwiches Luis's mother had carefully pinned to its bottom.

'No,' he corrected himself, prising them off and putting the flour sack on the scales again. 'Just within limits. *Just*.'

A weak cheer greeted this announcement. By now the general disappointment had begun to fade as, one by one, the members of 4C came to realize that, even if they didn't get to kick the flour babies about, there was consolation to be found in using Simon as a substitute. All around, his classmates had begun to take advantage of Simon's frozen misery to indulge in a barrage of hisses and jeers.

'Glorious Explosion, eh, Sime?'

'Wait till break-time!'

'We'll gloriously explode *you*!'

Mr Cartright kept on with his weighing, trying to ignore the cross-currents of disaffection and malevolence slewing about him. Not even having most of them in such a bad mood could stop his own spirits rising. As he called out each name, and dumped each flour sack in the shiny black bin bag, out of sight, he felt a weight dropping from him.

'Who's left?' he called out. 'Bill Simmons, do I have yours? Yes? Wayne, then.'

Wayne brought his flour baby up to the front.

'Looks a bit *thin*,' Mr Cartright said critically.

He threw the flour baby on the scales. The little steel pointer did its best, but, after a deal of desperate quivering, all it could manage was to struggle halfway across the scale.

'Three pounds, seven ounces!' Mr Cartright was incredulous. 'Only three pounds, seven ounces! Do you realize that this thing of yours has lost getting on for half its body weight?'

Wayne scowled so horribly that even Mr Cartright thought better of pursuing the matter.

And that left only one.

'Simon?'

Simon sat tight.

Mr Cartright looked up.

'Simon?' he said again.

Still Simon made no move. The boy looked ashen, Mr Cartright thought. Far more upset than could possibly be justified by the ring of hostile whispering around him. The boy was, after all, the most powerful member of the class by far. And fearless, too. If push came to shove, he could probably leave the whole pack of them lying bruised and battered on the pavement around him. So why on earth was he sitting there looking so wretched? Mr Cartright peered at him curiously. Could it be that he had truly believed all that nonsense about kicking the flour bags to pieces? Was this the sad snuffing of a glorious dream?

Really, if you thought about things too much, Mr Cartright decided, you could go quite unhinged, teaching 4C.

'Simon!' he bellowed. 'Get yourself and your flour baby up here. Now!'

Like someone in a deep trance, Simon stood up, dug in his school bag and pulled out the flour baby. Like a sleepwalker, he came up to the scales. Reluctantly, he handed her over.

Mr Cartright stared.

'What's this?'

Simon forced himself out of his reverie.

'Sir?'

Mr Cartright prodded the flour baby. Her bonnet promptly fell off, and she looked up at him at a distinctly rakish angle out of one badly smudged eye.

'What's this?' Mr Cartright repeated.

Simon was baffled.

'It's my flour baby, sir.'

Mr Cartright's look turned to one of dark displeasure.

'But it's *disgusting*,' he thundered. 'It's utterly revolting. It's in the most disgraceful state. It's an absolute *outrage*.'

'She did get a little bit grubby,' Simon admitted.

'Little bit grubby?' Mr Cartright lifted the flour baby by one of its corners. 'This isn't grubby. This is *black*.'

'Not exactly *bl* –'

But Mr Cartright didn't give him the chance to argue.

'I don't know how you have the nerve to bring this travesty, this *disgrace,* up to my desk.' He turned the flour baby over. 'And what's all this?' he roared. 'Burn! Toffee! Mud! Glue! Dribble!'

'It's not *my* dribble, sir,' Simon hastened to point out. He was all set to embark on his prepared indictment of Macpherson when he realized it was too late. Mr Cartright had reached flashpoint. While everyone else in the room settled back in their seats to relish Simon's discomfiture, Mr Cartright leaned over his desk, and stuck his angry face closer.

'I've put up with a good deal from you already this term,' he shouted at Simon. 'I've put up with your dark mulligrubs, and your mucking about in Assembly, and your continual persecution of poor Miss Arnott. But if you think for one moment I am going to put up with being handed back this – this –'

He lifted the flour baby and shuddered.

'This revolting little horror bag –'

He held it over the waste bin.

'Then you are wrong. Quite wrong.'

The flour baby trembled in his angry grip as she hung, sagging and dishevelled, over whatever sticky remnants of food had recently been spat out under orders.

Simon's eyes widened with panic. He couldn't drop her in there. *Surely* he couldn't.

He could, and did.

In a flash, with one of those lightning moves that kept him on the team, Simon had made the save. As Mr Cartright dropped the little sack of flour and turned away in irritation and disgust, Simon's hands shot out and caught it. And with a simultaneous access of quick thinking, he kicked the waste bin, hard.

'There!' Mr Cartright said, satisfied at what he took to

be the clang of flour baby in waste bin. 'Now can we get on with some work, please?'

He picked up a stump of chalk, and started scratching away on the blackboard. Hastily, Simon stuffed the flour baby up his jumper and turned back to face the class. No one seemed to have noticed his sleight of hand and foot. Good. They were all still glaring at him, certainly. But as he stumbled back to his seat, no one reached out and poked or grabbed at the tell-tale bulge in his sweater. For the moment, she was safe.

Simon collapsed on to his chair, and tried to pay attention to Mr Cartright.

'I'm writing names up here,' he was telling them sternly. 'The names of everyone who still has days missing from his flour baby diary. I don't care if you find them, rewrite them, or make them up. But everyone is to hand in enough for eighteen days.'

Not surprisingly, given its length, the list took some time to chalk up on the blackboard. While his classmates were busy watching out for their names, and, by extension, the chance for a noisy and protracted wrangle about the precise number of entries that were actually missing, Simon managed to smuggle his flour baby, completely unnoticed, out from under his sweater into the safe haven of his desk.

Mr Cartright wrote the last name – Rick Tullis – up very neatly in the top left hand corner, well out of the way, since the chances were high it would stay there.

Then he turned round.

'Anyone who finishes,' he consoled them, 'may go off to the library and do some private study.'

The general aura of resentment cleared a little at this announcement. One or two of them even cheered up enough to punch their fists in the air. For most of the members of 4C, the words 'private study' were generally taken to be synonymous with 'have a good laugh'.

Only George Spalder still seemed dissatisfied.

'But what about the snoopers?'

'Snoopers?'

'Yes, sir. Surely you're going to tell us who the snoopers were.'

'Snoopers ...'

A feeling of unease crept over Mr Cartright. Snoopers ... Picking up Dr Feltham's huge Science Fair memorandum, he turned to the page of rules in order to refresh his memory, and his eye fell on the one claiming that certain people – parents, pupils, staff, or even members of the public – would secretly be checking on the flour babies.

He wasn't supposed to have done anything about that, was he?

Mr Cartright turned over a page and saw the number in the top corner – 84. He turned back a page. Number 81. Not the sort of error Dr Feltham would make. A man who could spin round the school not only correcting the mistakes in everyone else's mental arithmetic, but also pointing out how they came to make the error in the first place, must know how to number pages correctly. Why, even Mr Cartright could *count*.

Gently, carefully, fearfully, Mr Cartright picked at the uncommonly thick page in question to find that, as he suspected, the hidden pages numbered 82 and 83 peeled apart, revealing detailed instructions for the teacher on the recruitment and supervision of out-of-class observers.

Snapping the memorandum shut, Mr Cartright said firmly to George:

'Oh, I don't think we need worry our heads about the snoopers.'

George couldn't have disagreed more strongly.

'You have to tell us who they *were*,' he insisted. 'So we can go out and bash them.'

It seemed that, on this issue at least, the whole class was in accord.

'Yes! Punch their lights out!'

'Rearrange their faces!'

'Give them a knuckle sandwich!'

Mr Cartright was reduced to cunning.

'I know,' he said. 'You make a list of everyone you think was snooping on you, and I'll tell you if you're right.'

They fell to the task with a will. And Mr Cartright was astonished to find each and every one of them labouring to write a list of a dozen or more badly-spelled names, to the accompaniment of a barrage of offensive remarks.

'I'm putting her down first. Nosy bat!'

'Prying old busybody! I don't think she took her beady eyes off me for a moment!'

'"Had your eyeful?" I asked him. "I don't even know what you're talking about", he said. But I *knew*. Oh, yes. I *knew*.'

Mr Cartright ambled round the class, watching in amazement as their lists of suspects grew longer and longer and their mutterings more and more baleful. It was extraordinary, he thought. And something to tell Dr Feltham. It was a waste of time recruiting real snoopers. There was clearly no need for that at all.

He walked past Tariq just as the boy was complaining venomously:

'Of course, they claimed they were just taking an interest. Anyone else would call it *meddling*.'

And the point was borne out in Bill Simmons' last diary entry.

Day 18

Good thing it's the last day because I couldn't stand any more prying and nagging. People with real babies must be totally soft targets if even flour babies make people you've never even met before come up and pretty well order you about. 'I shouldn't leave it there, dear. It might get muddy.' 'Don't you think you ought to bleh-bleh-bleh.' 'Shouldn't you bleh-bleh-bleh –

Mr Cartright reached down and lifted Bill Simmons' pen off the last *bleh*.

'Stuck in a groove?' he asked pleasantly. 'Allow me to help you.'

Ignoring Bill's poisonous look, he moved on to read Philip Brewster's last effort. Here again, the subject of snoopers was well to the fore.

What got me most about the flour babies was how sneaky people are. They go round pretending they're just being friendly and chatting to you, but really they're telling you you ought to be doing things differently. 'I'll tell you how I coped with mine,' they say, smiling creepily. Or, 'What I found worked best was this.' And you're supposed to smile back, and pretend you're so thick you haven't realized that they're telling you off.

And Sajid, as usual, cogently summed up the whole issue.

I'll tell you what I can't understand. You can hardly open the newspaper without reading about someone who's been arrested for bashing a baby, and it's never the first time they did it. I don't understand that, really I don't. I only had to give my flour baby a look, and my whole family was practically queuing up to phone the police and tell on me. So where do all these baby bashers live? Don't they have any family? Don't they have any neighbours? Don't they have any fr –

Sajid raised his head.

'How do you spell "friends"?' he asked of the room at large.

No reason not to try mending a fence or two, Simon thought, and spoke up.

'I think it's f-r-e-i-n-d-s. I wrote it that way a few minutes ago, and it looked quite all right to me.'

Dutifully, Mr Cartright strolled over the room to correct Simon's pitiful spelling. But before reaching down to despoil the last diary entry with his marking pen, he stood quietly behind the desk for a few moments, practising the skilled decoder's art.

Day 18. Over & Out.

So I was all wrong about the Glorious Explosion and getting to kick the flour babies to bits at the end. Who cares? I was planning on cheating anyway. I was going to hide mine, and join in battering everyone else's. I might be in 4C but I'm not absolutely stupid. I worked out days ago that I wouldn't be able to hurt mine, not any more, not now I've grown to like her. (And especially not now, when everyone hates me and I have no fr –

Mr Cartright was just leaning over, pen uncapped, to rearrange the next two vowels, when both of them disappeared before his eyes, dissolving in a miniature blue pool.

A teardrop. No doubt about it. And just like everything else about the boy, it was enormous. Hastily, before more could fall, Mr Cartright dug in his jacket pocket, fished out the huge spotted handkerchief, and thrust it into Simon's hand.

Simon stared down at the large blue blur on his work. No doubt about it. It was a teardrop. What was the matter with him? If he didn't get a grip, the others might notice. Come break-time, he would be *destroyed.*

Gratefully he took the handkerchief he was offered. And while Mr Cartright heaved his massive back end up on Simon's desk, deliberately shielding him from everyone's view, he tried to pull himself together.

When Mr Cartright felt the damp handkerchief pushed back in his hand, he took it that it was safe to slide off the desk, and carry on reading.

I really liked having that flour baby to look after, even though I got sick of her and she drove me mad. I liked seeing her sitting on top of the wardrobe watching me while I lay in bed at night. I liked chatting to her at breakfast. And I liked cuddling her to make Macpherson jealous. Last night, when I was rocking her in my arms, Mum said I reminded her of someone. She didn't say who, and I didn't have to ask. But it was good to know he used to rock me like that when I was a baby. Maybe he really did love me, in his way.

Quite forgetting, in the emotion of the moment, that the handkerchief had already been pressed into service more than once, Mr Cartright drew it out, and, lighting on a fairly dry patch, blew his nose in a trumpeting fashion. Then, bravely, he forced himself to read to the end.

He just wasn't very good at showing it, running away like that. But I can't talk, can I? My flour baby ended up such a mess, I practically got my ears torn off. But I really did care about her. I really did.

Mr Cartright could bear it no longer.

'For heaven's sake, lad,' he whispered hoarsely.

'If you love the thing that much, go and fish it out of the waste bin. Take it home.'

Simon said nothing. But, flushing scarlet, he unconsciously leaned forward and gripped the sides of his desk.

Slowly, suspiciously, Mr Cartright tipped Simon back a few inches, lifted the desk lid, and peered in.

The flour baby peered back at him anxiously, out of the dark.

Mr Cartright lowered the desk lid. He looked at Simon. Simon looked at him. Then Mr Cartright said:

'Do you want to know your problem, Simon Martin? You sell yourself too short. Your flour baby is a squalid and disgusting little creature. She wouldn't pass any hygiene tests, and, if she were real, she wouldn't win any Natty Baby competitions. But if keeping what you care for close and safe counts for anything, I'll tell you this. You'll make a better father than most.'

Then, clearing his throat loudly, he strode off as fast as he could, back to the sanctuary of his own desk.

Notes for Chapter 10

Simon's frustrations with the school system increase despite having had a more mature attitude to his learning recently. He keeps being in the wrong place at the wrong time and getting more and more detentions. As he grows in frustration he also begins to understand the difficulties and ties of having a baby and the reasons why his father may have left. The novel therefore ends with Simon's more personal problems resolved as he comes to an understanding of himself and his family.

What do you think?
Stop when you get to page 177 'Just get them out of this building! Now!'. What do you think might happen next?

Questions
1. 'With authority gone, the pack instantly went after their true quarry.' (page 168). Explain the meaning of this phrase and how the description is appropriate to the boys.
2. Why does Simon feel free and ecstatic?
3. Consider the last line of the book. Why is it so important?

Further activities
1. Piece together the song used in *Flour Babies* from Chapters 8 and 10. Can you explain its importance in the novel in relation to the following:
   - the actions of Simon's father
   - linking the character of Simon to that of his father
   - creating suspense
   - Mr Cartright's character
   - the theme of growing up
   - the issue of teenage parenthood.

2. Now you've finished the book, write your own review of it, if possible, in one of the following Internet sites: http://www.uk.bol.com and http://www.amazon.co.uk. Search for *Flour Babies* and then click on 'Write your own review'.

Chapter 10

Fired with determination to get the whole flour baby project out of the way for good, Mr Cartright kept everyone working. And as the clock hand rolled around the hour, interminably slowly, the sense of righteous outrage always felt by the members of 4C when sustained effort was expected of them merged with their resentment of Simon for his two terrible mistakes: picking the project in the first place, and being wrong about the Glorious Explosion.

For form's sake, Mr Cartright pretended he was deaf to the flurries of malignant whispering around him.

'What sort of *Warpo* chooses to do babies anyhow?'

'We could have chosen *any* of the others. We could have done *food*.'

To try and distract them, he picked up the sheet of paper Russ Mould had just pushed aside with a huge sigh of relief.

'Here. Someone's finished. Let me inspire the rest of you by reading out Russ's final entry.'

He held it in front of his eyes for a few moments, trying – and failing – to decipher it.

'You're holding it upside down,' Russ said reproachfully.

Hastily, Mr Cartright turned the page the other way up.

'Ah, yes!' he said. 'That's better.'

He peered at it for a few moments longer, concentrating hard, and then, defeated, gave it back to Russ.

'I wonder if you haven't been just a shade over-ambitious,' he suggested gently. 'Trying to move on to joined up writing quite so soon.'

As he stepped away, the bell rang, precipitating the usual frenzy of illicit bag-packing and chair-scraping.

'Wait till the voice goes green!' he roared.

The squall abated for a moment.

Mr Cartright decided to make for the staffroom, and his reviving cup of coffee, a few minutes ahead of the stampede. Imposing his will on the whole lot of them with the darkest of looks, he moved backwards to the door. Then,

'Right,' he said. 'Off you go.'

Before the words were even out of his mouth, he was away, down the long corridor.

With authority gone, the pack instantly went after their true quarry.

'Thought you could get away with it, did you, Sime?'

'Leading us on like that!'

'"Best science I've ever heard", you told us. "Dead brilliant", you said.'

Once again, Simon unconsciously leaned forward and gripped his desk. No one believed the gesture stemmed from fear, and so for the second time that morning it proved his undoing.

'What have you got in there?'

'Open up, Sime!'

'Let's see!'

They were too many for him. Their combined weight,

and the enthusiastic charge, toppled the desk and sent the lid flying open.

The flour baby shot out and sailed over the energetically fighting scrum. She flew high over the abandoned desks. Simon skidded beneath, tracking her flight, and managed to catch her, puffing flour from every pore, just as Mr Cartright came back to fetch his cigarettes.

Striding to his desk, Mr Cartright took a brief, irritable look at the disorder and the small cloud of flour settling on the far side of the room. After wasting time retracing his steps, he wasn't in the mood to fritter away more of his precious break pursuing either truth or justice.

It was Simon he blamed.

'Monday detention!' he boomed. 'For starting an unruly ball game in my classroom.'

Lifting the desk lid a few inches, he surreptitiously drew the tell-tale cigarette packet out from its hiding place under some papers in the corner. Then, seeing they were all trying to work out why he'd come back, he made a show of grasping the bin bag of flour babies, and dragging it out of the door behind him.

Simon stood staring at his departing back, outraged by the sheer injustice of the punishment. Sensing his temporary loss of concentration, Wayne dived for the flour baby. Without thinking twice, Simon spun round and hurled her in the air, giving himself enough time to leap on the seat of a chair, catch her safely, and hold her out of Wayne's reach.

Hearing the scuffle from halfway down the corridor, Mr

Cartright strode back and caught Simon standing on the chair.

'Tuesday detention!' he bellowed. 'For climbing on school property.'

Again, he turned to go.

Simon stood, encircled and besieged, as the rest of 4C crept closer, bent on the capture of his flour baby. Should he leap for the door now, before they expected him to make a move? They knew as well as he did that Mr Cartright would hear him pounding the other way down the corridor, whip round, and give him yet another detention for running within the school building.

But so what? Marooned on his chair, holding the flour baby high, Simon couldn't help thinking it. So *what?* There were worse things in life than getting three detentions in a row. Why, even added up, they wouldn't last longer than one of Hyacinth Spicer's grisly birthday parties, and he'd survived seven of those.

So maybe he should just go for it. Give it a whirl. What had Old Carthorse said? '*Aren't you supposed to be one of the school's sporting heroes?*'

Yes, go for it!

In a rush of exhilaration, Simon suddenly astonished everyone around him by leaping for the door. The noise was tremendous. From desk to desk he leaped, leaving wobbly wooden legs rattling frantically, and chairs keeling over backwards. He held the flour baby high, and, as he jumped, what Mr Cartright said rang in his ears. '*Do you want to know your problem. Simon Martin? You sell yourself too short.*' He sprang from Wayne's desk to Russ's in a clatter of flying pens and rulers. He sent Philip Brewster's calculator flying. He vaulted over Luis's desk entirely. And with one last tremendous bound, he made it to safety. He was through the door, punching the air with a fist. He felt as powerful as when, all those years ago, Miss Ness pinned the wonderful scarlet cloak around him for the nativity play, and he could practically hear trumpets. Who'd make a bad father? Not him, for sure. Maybe people like Robin Foster couldn't stand the pace, and ended up putting an early end to their responsibilities. And people like Sue never even dared risk it. But as for him, Simon Martin, he wouldn't be bad at all. In fact, he'd be *better* than not bad. He'd be pretty *good*. In a glorious, glorious explosion of confidence, the words Mr Cartright said echoed mightily in his brain. '*If keeping what you care for close and safe counts for anything, you'll make a better father than most.*'

The foot stuck out to trip him brought him down. He landed with a thud and a grunt, and lay, spreadeagled and winded, as the flour baby shot out of his hands, and slid twenty feet along the corridor.

The real voice put instant flight to the echo.

'Ah! Simon Martin! Just the boy I need. Wednesday detention, of course, for running in the corridor. But, since you're here, would you be so good as to drag this bag along to Dr Feltham's Science Fair? There's a good lad.'

And, patting the comforting little packet in his jacket

pocket, Mr Cartright hurried off for his coffee and a quick smoke.

Simon had just hauled himself painfully into a sitting position when Dr Feltham spun around the corner with a bevy of helpers in tow, carrying the various parts of the Hughes twins' hydro-electric power station.

'Back! Back, back, back!' Like a lion tamer, Dr Feltham snarled at the bulk of 4C who were fighting their way through the doorway after Simon. 'Get back, boys! Back at once! Can't you see this is expensive equipment?'

No sooner had he said the words 'expensive equipment' than he noticed Wishart's Digital Sine-Wave Generator on the floor where, on Mr Cartright's orders, Simon had abandoned it earlier.

'What on earth?'

Then he saw the oscilloscope lying beside the radiator.

'This is outrageous!'

Then he saw Simon.

'You! You there, boy! Lounging about on the floor! You!'

Aware of the crippling limitations of speech, Simon simply hung his head.

'Monday detention!' Dr Feltham ordered.

'I'm booked up till Wednesday.' Simon told him sourly.

'Thursday, then!' snapped Dr Feltham. 'Now look sharp! That equipment should have been taken through to the laboratories well over an hour ago.'

Sighing, Simon scrambled to his feet, and looked round for someone to help him. But everyone in 4C had disappeared. Simon presumed, bitterly and rightly, that they had prudently begun to melt away the instant Dr Feltham started firing on all cylinders and dishing out punishment detentions. So taking off only a moment to make a horrible face at his tormentor's back, Simon thrust his own flour baby safely back up his jumper, and gathered up Wishart's Digital Sine-Wave Generator and the oscilloscope. After shifting them about a bit, he managed to find a way of carrying both that left a few fingers free. With these, he grasped the neck of the heavy-duty bin bag, and slowly, slowly, stumbled backwards along the corridor, still balancing the equipment in his arms.

He found Mr Higham standing in wait behind the third set of swing doors in the science block.

'About time!' He snatched the oscilloscope from Simon. 'This should have been here well over an hour ago!'

He consulted the massive Science Fair display plan Dr Feltham had pinned to the wall.

'That thing of Wishart's goes in here as well.'

As he lifted the Digital Sine-Wave Generator out of Simon's arms, he noticed the third and last burden.

'What's in that bin bag?'

'Flour babies.'

Mr Higham took another look at the master plan.

'Flour babies ... flour babies ... Ah! Here we are!' His face crumpled into a frown. 'Bit *early*, aren't they? Oh, never mind. Display on Table 18.'

In vain he waited for Simon to make a move.

'Go on, then,' he repeated impatiently. 'Go and display them.'

Simon scowled. He was sick of people snapping at him.

'How?' he asked sullenly.

But Mr Higham had a bigger fish to fry. Pitkin's Electronic Window Burglar Alarm was just being carried through the door.

'For heaven's sake, boy!' he scolded Simon. 'Do you have to be *spoonfed*? Just set the things out to look interesting, and write a label explaining what they are.'

So Simon grudgingly dragged the bin bag over to Table 18, which, he couldn't help noticing with a flicker of resentment, was the one hidden away furthest in the corner. He pulled out the flour babies one by one, and dumped them on the table. Looking at each in turn, he was aware for the first time how much most of them had changed over the last eighteen days. His was no longer the only one with eyes. Several had noses, ears, lips, and even warts. George Spalder's appeared to have measles. Bill Simmons' sported one of his speciality bluebottle tattoes. Luis's even had a pipe.

Now what would make an interesting display?

First. Simon pulled his own flour baby out from under his jumper and set her in the middle of the table. Then he put all the others in a circle round her.

Good.

He took a label from a nearby table and turned it over to the blank side.

'*Queen Flour Baby and her Courtiers*', he wrote, then looked at it critically. Even if people could make out what it said, they wouldn't find it interesting.

He tried again. This time he divided the flour babies into pairs, and tried to set them in the sorts of positions that suggested a Saturday night party.

He stole the card from another table. Crossing out the neatly printed words *Measuring the Wavelength of Laser Light*, he turned it over and tried to write:

Orgy.

Only four letters, and yet he suspected that at least two of them were wrong, or badly out of place. And, anyway, it didn't look a very interesting party. He tried to liven it up a bit by moving the flour babies into more interesting positions. But somehow they still managed to persist in looking disappointingly like eighteen little sacks of flour, just lying in a jumble on the table.

Giving up, Simon tried something different. This time he set them out in strict rows and wrote *Dr Feltham's Class of Ear'oles* on yet another card.

Not very interesting.

His next idea was the best. Taking the card belonging to Hocking's Zero Gravity Project, he wrote on the back: *Simon Martin's Greatest Goal Ever.* And then he set to recreating it with the help of the flour babies and a chocolate bar wrapper he found on the floor and crumpled up for a football.

First he put the front three players into place. Then the middle four, and then the back three. Then he put in the other team. He'd played deep in defence, that glorious day. But when the time came, he'd dribbled the ball up the wing in an astonishing spurt of speed, swerving to miss one defender after another. He'd reached the edge of the penalty area, and let fly such a kick that the ball shot straight in the corner of the net. The goalie didn't even see it, and Simon didn't have the time to swing away from the inevitable collision with their beefy, cross-eyed sweeper.

Taken up with the memory, he ran through the last moves of play, propelling the flour babies.

'Baroom! Baroom! Pow!'

As the two sacks collided, flour puffed out and showered all over.

Out of the way the table might have been. Invisible it wasn't. Mr Higham had stormed over within seconds.

'Flour! You're getting flour over everything! What's the matter with you, Simon Martin? Why are you acting even more like a half-wit than usual?'

Simon was nettled. He had, after all, only been doing his best to follow orders.

Mr Higham spun round like a frenzied top.

'Look!' he was shouting. 'Look at all this flour! It's settling on Bernstein's Pressurized Cylinders! And Butterworth's Speech Synthesis machine! You can take a detention for this, Simon Martin.'

'Friday's my earliest,' Simon informed him in a voice that was icy with resentment.

'Friday, then! And don't think I won't be in to check on you. I'll –'

Mr Higham broke off.

'My God! Now it's drifting down into Tugwell's Purified Water apparatus!'

He turned to Simon.

'Get those things out of here!'

'But –'

'Get them out!'

Mr Higham was in such a fury that Simon didn't argue. Hastily, he shovelled all the flour babies, including his own, into the bin bag.

'Hurry up! Quick! Get them out of here! Take them away!'

Still scowling, Simon dragged the bin bag towards the door.

'But where shall I – ?'

Mr Higham was in no mood to solve Simon's problem.

'Just get them out! Take them away! I don't care if you kick the damn things to bits. Just get them out of this building! Now!'

Obediently, Simon dragged the heavy bin bag out of the door and back past the other laboratories. He was in no mood to take care going through the swing doors, and the bag snagged on one set of floor catches after another. The trail of flour he was leaving behind grew wider and deeper with each step.

He'd reached the main door out of the science block when he ran into Miss Arnott.

'What are you doing out of class?' she asked. 'The bell rang for the end of break several minutes ago.'

Simon considered. He could have claimed that he was taking the flour babies to the science block. But it was unlikely that Miss Arnott would believe him, since he was clearly off the other way.

He could claim he was taking them back to his own classroom. But she was more than capable of watching till he'd gone through the door. And, like messengers of old who brought bad news and were killed for their pains, Simon seriously doubted the wisdom of being the one to bring the flour babies back to Mr Cartright.

Or he could say nothing, as usual.

He said nothing, as usual.

Miss Arnott patted her shoulder bag, to check she still had her bottle of aspirins with her.

'I'm sorry, Simon, but I have no choice. If you don't have a reason to be out of class, I'm forced to give you a detention.'

'It will have to be Monday week,' Simon warned her. 'I'm fully booked till then.'

'Oh, Simon!' said Miss Arnott, pressing the points on her temple where her headaches always started.

'It's all right,' Simon assured her valiantly. 'I don't mind.' And it was true. Between trying to explain, and taking another detention, he much preferred the detention. It was easier.

'Monday week, then.'

Like an unseasonal Santa, Simon nodded, gripped the bin bag, and moved off grimly down the corridor. Miss Arnott stepped aside to let him pass.

And saw the trail of flour.

'Simon –'

'Yes, Miss Arnott?'

But she had gone, fleeing to the staffroom to get some water for her aspirins. Simon stood looking at her footprints down the flour. Something – call it prescience, call it second sight – warned him Miss Arnott wouldn't be with them very much longer. The woman was losing her grip, that was quite obvious. And if there was one thing you needed to be a teacher, it was grip. You needed it from a quarter past eight in the morning till a quarter past four at night. He stopped to count the hours on his fingers. Eight. It sounded a major grind, but, when you came to think, it was only a third of each day. Eight measly hours. If poor Miss Arnott couldn't even manage that, then she'd better not leave and have a baby.

Now there was a *real* job, thought Simon. Twenty-four hour shifts. Every day. For nearly twenty years. No breaks. No holidays. It made one of Hyacinth's parties look like a mayfly's quick blink. Being a parent was pretty well a life sentence. Why, if instead of going off to hospital to have a baby all those years ago, his mother had stabbed someone to death with a bread knife, she'd be out of gaol by now. Twice over, probably, if she'd been good.

Simon tugged his own flour baby out of the bin bag and stared at her. The more you thought about it, the more extraordinary it was, this business of having babies. No doubt about it, it was dangerous. It slowed you up. It tied you down. It cramped your style. It brought out the spy and the nag in everyone around you. And it made being a teacher look like party-time. No wonder his father hadn't been able to stick it. How had he even lasted a thousand and eight hours? That was twice as long as Simon had looked after his flour baby. And look at his mother! Her score was up in the hundreds of thousands already! She must be a real *heroine*. She must be a *saint*.

'She must be absolutely sick of me,' he told the flour baby.

But it wasn't true, and he knew it. The words even rang a little hollowly down the corridor. Because Simon knew in his heart that, give or take the odd day when he'd done something truly daft like feeding Gran's wig to Tullis's alsatian, or throwing that cactus at Hyacinth, she was quite fond of him really. That was the problem.

'That's how the trap works,' he explained to the flour baby. 'That's how it gets you. First you know nothing. Then it's far too late.'

He paused.

'Unless you're a tall ship.'

A tall ship …

His father …

Simon sat down on the bin bag, which bulged voluptuously beneath his weight, and formed a snug nest around him. He was thinking hard.

His father.

Experimentally, he rolled the words out, considering them in a new way.

'My father. My father. My father.'

'Who?'

'*Who*?'

'*Who*?'

The live echo was Robin, sent to track him down, and bring him back for a roasting.

'Exactly!' said Simon. '*Who*?'

But Robin was in no mood for riddles. He was on a mission.

'Out of that bag, Sime. Time to get back to base. Old Carthorse is smouldering in his socks.'

'You see,' explained Simon, ignoring him totally. 'I don't know who he is. And he doesn't know who I am. And so what Mum and Gran say is quite right. The fact that he walked out is really nothing to do with me.'

'Out of the bag, Sime! Time's up!'

'I'm not saying what he did was *right*,' Simon went on. 'Sailing off like that and leaving my mum to look after me for ever and ever.' He poked the flour baby. 'Though after lugging this thing about for three weeks, I can understand how it happened. I'm just saying that it shouldn't – doesn't – matter to me any longer.'

'Yes, Sime. Now out of the bag, *please*.'

'You see, I'm finished with him,' Simon persisted. 'In fact, in a way, we never even started. He's really nothing at all to do with me. And out there in the world there are millions and millions of people who have nothing to do with me, who don't even know me. They all get on perfectly well without me. And I get on perfectly well without them.'

But Robin's patience had run out.

'Sime, I'm not getting in trouble for you. I'm going back now. I'm going to tell Old Carthorse I found you but you wouldn't come. You were too busy sitting in a flour bag, spouting about your family.'

It was as if Simon didn't even hear him.

'And what I've realized is that my father is just one more person on the planet who doesn't know who I am. That's all he is. And only the people who know you really count.'

'*I'm* counting, Sime.'

'And so my mother counts. And Gran. And Sue.'

'One …'

'But not him. He doesn't count.'

'Two …'

'Not that I'm blaming him. But he doesn't count.'

'Three!'

Despairing of forcing Simon to see sense, Robin turned to go back to the classroom. And as he reached the bend in the corridor, he could still hear faintly, from behind, the sound of Simon holding forth to his flour baby.

'I feel a lot better now, really I do. I don't think I knew how much the whole business has been bothering me. But I feel different now. I feel *free*.'

The flour baby stared back out of her sympathetic, long-lashed eyes.

'You do *see*, don't you?'

The look on her face never altered.

'You *understand*?'

The flour baby watched him impassively.

And slowly, inexorably, Simon came back to his senses. What was he *doing*, sitting in a school corridor in a nice, comfy bin bag, chatting to a lump of flour? Was he *cracked*?

Simon leaped to his feet as if he'd been scalded. Flour baby! She wasn't a flour baby. She was a silly, lifeless bag of flour. She wasn't even a *she*. She was an it. What was the *matter* with him? For nearly three weeks now, he'd been discussing his life with a flour sack. Was he *unhinged*? This thing he was holding was nothing more than part of some boring school project. She wasn't real. *None* of them were real.

Grasping the corners of the bin bag, he upended it forcibly. Flour sacks spilled far and wide. That's all they were. Flour sacks! Sacks of flour!

Picking one up, he hurled it at the ceiling. It split, showering flour all over. Simon didn't care. He felt the most extraordinary relief, as if he'd suddenly been let out of gaol; as if, swimming hopelessly round and round after a shipwreck, he'd spotted lights on land; as if the doctor and the vicar and the teacher had come to tell him they were wrong, just a mistake, he wasn't going to have to be a parent yet after all.

It was all over. The relief of it! He hurled another flour baby. And another. Because it had been a near thing, a very near thing. He'd really grown to love his flour baby. He'd really cared about her. But she wasn't real! And so he was free! Free, free, *free*!

The next flour baby caught on the light fitting and tore. Ecstatically, Simon lifted his face to the cascade of flour spilling down on him, and hurled the next flour baby harder. Why should he care? Hadn't Mr Higham all but given him permission, after all? *'I don't care if you kick the damn things to bits. Just get them out of here.'* And Simon had.

Kick them to bits, though?

Great idea!

He kicked one, and then another. Flour exploded all over. It billowed down the corridor in mushrooming white clouds. Each time he kicked another flour sack, more huge puffs of pure white transformed the dull corridor into a storm of snow, a dazzling blizzard – a glorious, glorious explosion.

The flour was drifting up the walls, and settling ankle-deep. Who cared? Not huge, white, flour-kicking Simon. There would be time enough to be responsible when he was older. When the right moment came, there would be all the time in the world to be a good father.

But not now. Not while he was so young. Not while he had the strength and power and energy to do anything, and all his horizons were giddy and bright, and wider than he could imagine.

Boot ... Boot ... As flour flurried and swirled in arctic chaos, Simon raised his arms to it in triumph. He wouldn't make the same mistake as his father. Oh, no. He wasn't going to pin himself down years too soon, and have to make the bitter choice between snatching back his own life, and leaving some child to dawdle down Wilberforce Road every day, talking inside his head to some crinkly blue-eyed father he'd had to make up all by himself, because the real one hadn't stayed around.

He'd never do that. Never, never, never. He'd wait till he was ready. He'd take care. And then, one day maybe, when he felt like it …

Boot … Boot …

Flour rained on him. It ran all over him in rills and rivulets. It swirled all about him. He was a snowman, a yeti, a walking avalanche. *Boot … Boot …* He took all the petty frustrations of three weeks out on the tattered bags of flour. 'Don't leave her there, Sime.' 'Be careful.' 'Are you sure she's safe?' Is this what his Mum was feeling all those years ago, when she dragged him down the club so she could let fly playing badminton one measly hour a week? How *could* he have leaned over the balcony nagging at her like that? How *could* he?

Boot … Boot … Boot … More bags split and showered flour. His mother was a *saint.* He'd take her flowers. He'd bully Sajid into lending some of his ill-gotten gains, and he'd take his Mum a dozen red roses. She deserved them.

Simon dipped his arms elbow deep in flour, and, ripping the last few flour babies apart at the seams, he shook the flour all over. He was so happy, nothing could spoil it. They could give him detentions till hell froze. He didn't care. An hour a day? Chicken-feed! Look at what he'd just escaped!

He couldn't help it. He burst into song.

'Unfurl the sail, lads, and let the winds find me
Breasting the soft sunny, blue rising main –'

The strong voice rang out in the storm of flour. Scooping up more handfuls, he tossed them around him, white on white. Oh, lucky, lucky Simon!

'Toss all my burdens and woes clear behind me,' he carolled.
'Vow I'll not carry those cargoes again.'

The flour gusted round him like a good sou'wester.

'Sail for a sunrise that burns with new maybes –'

Louder and louder he sang. He wasn't trapped. He would be punished, but he wasn't trapped. And there'd be time enough to be responsible.

'Farewell, my loved ones, and be of good cheer.'

There weren't many bits of sacking left now. The flour spread all the way down to the corner. A pity about there being nothing at all by 4C in the Science Fair. Still, never mind. At least they'd learned a lot.

The matchless voice soared.

'Others may settle to dandle their babies –'

With one last kick at the flour, Simon set off down the corridor.

'My heart's a tall ship, and high winds are near.'

Martin Simon, taking the opportunity of a trip to the lavatories to finish the last pages of *The Quest for the Holy Grail*, lifted his head from the words he was reading.

'Here is the source of valour undismayed,' he couldn't help repeating, whispering it softly to himself. For it did seem that here in front of him was someone magically tall and

strong, who walked like a knight in his aura of pure white – awesome and amazing.

Martin Simon flattened himself against the wall as Simon Martin strode past, singing.

And Mr Cartright, testily making his way along the corridor to fetch his errant pupil, heard the glorious, glorious tenor voice echoing from ceiling and walls, and fell back respectfully to let the young vision in white sail past, like a tall ship, out into his unfettered youth.

Further reading

All the following books can be found in paperback, or in your local library.

Other novels by Anne Fine

Crummy Mummy and Me (Puffin, 1989)
Mina has a difficult time trying to make her mother act sensibly and responsibly. This mother dyes her hair blue, wears fishnet tights and is certainly no ordinary mother. In fact the whole family is pretty unusual and once again we see Anne Fine exploring the family and relationships.

Bill's New Frock (Longman, 1992)
Bill wakes up to find he's turned into a girl. He's forced to wear a pink dress and is not allowed to play football. In this lively comedy Anne Fine explores how girls and boys are treated differently.

Madame Doubtfire (Longman, 1996)
This is the book on which the Robin Williams' film, *Mrs Doubtfire*, was based. It is a book which focuses on a father, his relationship with his children and how far he'll go to be with them. When Miranda advertises for a cleaning lady, her ex-husband, Daniel, disguises himself and manages to secure the job!

The Book of the Banshee (Longman, 1997)
How do you cope when your household is completely dominated by your sister's terrible teenage tantrums? This book focuses on the theme of growing up and is set at school and at Will Flowers' house, which seems to have turned into a war zone ... a war between his sister and everyone else in the house.

The Tulip Touch (Longman, 1999)

Tulip might seem violent and cruel to everyone else, but Natalie is friends with her and wants to defend her. At first she finds her exciting, that is, until her games become more and more sinister, and Natalie realises she is going too far.

Step by Wicked Step (Puffin, 1996)

A creepy tale which follows a group of children thrown together in the tower of dark and sinister Harwick Hall. There they find the diary of a Victorian teenager which tells of his wicked stepfather. Each of the children tells their own story about divorce, step-parents and the experience of living in the modern step-family.

Goggle-Eyes (Longman, 1996)

Kitty Killin tells the story of her life with her mother's boyfriend Gerald, whom she hates. This is another book which addresses the issues of stepchildren, stepparents and new relationships.

An Interview with Anne Fine (Mammoth, 1999)

This non-fiction book is part of a series of interviews with popular children's authors. Anne Fine talks about her pet hates, school experiences, family and writing novels.

Novels with similar themes by other authors

Buddy by Nigel Hinton (Puffin, 1994)

A book which looks at the confusions of being a teenager in a thoughtful and often amusing way. Buddy is embarrassed by his father who is more interested in dreaming of his Teddy-boy youth, listening to old records and a life of crime, than taking on the real responsibilities of parenthood.

The Daydreamer by Ian McEwan (Red Fox, 1995)

A thought-provoking book in which the main character, Peter, cannot help himself from leaving reality and entering the wild world of his imagination. Through his dreams, Ian McEwan explores relationships in the family and the experience of growing up. We follow Peter's imagination as he swaps bodies with the family cat and is locked into the body of a baby he hates.

The Turbulent Term of Tyke Tiler by Gene Kemp (Puffin, 1984)
A lively book which explores the pranks and escapades of Tyke Tiler, which, like *Flour Babies,* is set mainly in school. Danny Price, who is no academic, joins forces with Tyke, and together they cause mayhem in their last term at Cricklepitt Combined School.

Dear Nobody by Berlie Doherty (Lions, 1993)
A play which explores teenage pregnancy and the difficulties that go with this responsibility. Helen and Chris are in their last year at school when Helen becomes pregnant. While she wants to finish the relationship, Chris wants to be involved in the plans for the baby.

You will find an interesting site on the Internet, which is related to the text: *Dear Nobody* by Berlie Doherty, at http://www.bbc.co.uk/education/dear_nobody, which includes true stories about young parents as well as facts and links to other useful sites. This might be useful for some of your work on *Flour Babies*.

Scarecrows by Robert Westall (Puffin, 1995)
Another gripping book which focuses on the experience of growing up in a difficult household. Simon values the memory of his father who was killed on duty as a soldier. He hates his new stepfather as a result. Here Westall combines this family setting with a more horrifying twist, as the three scarecrows that appear in the field near the house seem to be moving nearer and nearer to them each night.

Programme of study

The battle of wits between Mr Cartright and 4C

Look at the passage beginning 'Satisfied that honours were now even ...' on page 30 and ending 'Let chaos reign' on page 37. Then answer questions from page 191 to page 196.

Word

1. A common word in this text is the plural noun 'babies'. Turn the nouns below into their plural forms, thinking carefully about spelling:

Singular noun	plural noun
baby	
worry	
lorry	
ferry	
curry	
story	
discovery	
activity	
jetty	
folly	
day	
bay	
ray	
key	
boy	

From the exercise above can you work out the rule that will help you remember when to add –s and when to add –ies?

2. Anne Fine chooses adverbs carefully to help us understand more about characters and their reactions to events in the novel. Look at the sentences below and underline the adverbs. Then explain what the adverb suggests about the thoughts and behaviour of the particular character it refers to. The first one is done for you.

(a) 'Simon sucked air in <u>sharply</u> between his teeth.'
    The adverb suggests that Simon makes a noise with the air between his teeth and that he is annoyed with Mr Cartright cunningly trying to manipulate the class.
(b) '"Old Smoothy-chops!" he muttered bitterly to his neighbour at the next desk.'
(c) 'Mr Cartright beamed brightly and asked,
    '"Now who'd prefer textiles?"'
(d) 'Inwardly, Mr Cartright shuddered.
    '"Tell you what," he said brightly. "Let's not bother with textiles."'
(e) '"You're let off down the shops in consumer studies," he threatened Mr Cartright darkly.'
(f) 'Luis gazed round the room proudly.'
(g) '"You must be making all this up," Mr Cartright accused them sternly.'

3. Early in this section, Mr Cartright uses speech cleverly to attempt to persuade the boys not to choose the flour babies' project. Look at the following phrases and underline the words or phrases that he uses to form a persuasive argument. Comment on how he is using language to persuade the boys not to do the flour babies' project. The first three are done for you:

(a) '<u>I'm</u> a <u>reasonable</u> man': Mr Cartright assures the class he is reasonable by saying 'I'm'. He makes himself out to be friendly and fair so that they respect his opinion and think kindly towards him.
(b) '<u>there's no reason why</u> you should all suffer': Mr Cartright tries to make himself appear kind and caring by saying he doesn't want them to 'suffer'.

(c) 'we'll explain to him about the principles': Mr Cartright uses the word 'we' to link himself with the boys, as if they are all working together towards one goal, and are united.

(d) 'we can let bygones be bygones'

(e) 'who'd prefer textiles?'

(f) 'Let's not bother with textiles. Let's just make it consumer studies instead.'

(g) 'You realise … that only leaves babies and food.'

(h) 'Surely a growing lad like you enjoys the odd plate of extra fodder.'

Sentence

1. Look at the following sentences and punctuate them accurately into direct speech. The first one is done for you:

(a) 'You must be making all this up,' Mr Cartright accused them sternly.

(b) Quieter than that Simon responded virtuously

(c) That's right sir Robin Foster backed Simon up

(d) What about the rest of you interrupted Mr Cartright

(e) Old Smoothy-chops he muttered bitterly to his neighbour at the next desk Robin Foster. He's just trying to wriggle out of the flour babies because they're the *best*.

2. Look at the section of the text (pages 31–32) where Anne Fine gives the direct speech of the boys shouting out to Mr Cartright about textiles. She does not tell us who is shouting each phrase. Just like Mr Cartright himself, the reader cannot tell who is shouting out.

• Write a list of synonyms for the verb 'said'. The list has been started for you below:

shouted   murmured
bawled   muttered
snarled

- Pick six of these substitute words for 'said' that would be most appropriate for the classroom Anne Fine is describing. Write out the passage and add them to the dialogue, along with the person's name who might have said it. Think carefully about the punctuation. The first one is done for you:

  'Sewing and stuff! Great! You watch out, Foster! I owe you a good stabbing with the unpicker, back from first year,' bawled Wayne.

3. As Mr Cartright talks about domestic economy the boys complain about always writing and choosing recipes. Have a look at a recipe and see if you can answer the following questions about this convention of writing:

   - Write out the title of the recipe you have looked at.
   - What sections would you expect to find in the text of a recipe?
   - Write out five verbs that are used in the instructions.
   - Can you identify the form of the verbs?

Text

1. At the beginning of Chapter 2, the boys in the class seemed the victims of the school system, not being given the chance to do well and be valued by their teacher. In this passage do you still view them as victims of Mr Cartright? Give reasons for your answer.

2. Skim-read from the beginning of the passage to 'Why had schools been invented, for heaven's sake?' on page 33, looking carefully for language and imagery that likens the boys to animals. Look also for language to do with violence and fighting. Write out these words and phrases and explain why you think Anne Fine is using this language to describe the situation.

3. In this section Anne Fine allows us to understand the situation from two viewpoints: Mr Cartright's and Simon's. Pick one

quotation from the text that illustrates Mr Cartright's point of view and one that illustrates Simon's.

4. Look at the following essay question and writing frame.

'Why had schools been invented, for heaven's sake?' Examine how school, teachers and education are portrayed in *Flour Babies*.

For each paragraph you have been given a topic sentence. You will need to do the following:
- finish off the introduction, giving your reader a brief overview of the story
- expand on each point made, showing your knowledge of the story
- add a quotation to prove your point
- comment on the quotation.

Introduction: Flour Babies is a novel written by Anne Fine. It tells the story of a boy called Simon Martin who finds school difficult and is unhappy about the fact that his father left him when he was a baby. The story focuses on a school project run with his class where the boys have to look after a bag of flour for 21 days as if it were a baby. The purpose of the project is to ...

  (a) The novel explores the experiences of a class of students who find lessons difficult. It opens with a description of poor behaviour in Mr Cartright's lesson. The class is full of interesting characters and there are many possible reasons for their behaviour ...

  (b) Anne Fine shows us a contrasting experience of school through the character of Martin Simon ...

  (c) Their science teacher is Mr Cartright. He is quite a strict teacher ...

  (d) Anne Fine shows a contrasting teacher in Dr Feltham ...

  (e) Miss Arnott is another teacher described in the novel ...

  (f) Simon's feelings about school change throughout the novel ...

(g) Anne Fine explores the theme of education by looking at not only academic learning, but learning about life and the real world. The purpose of the project was to teach the boys about themselves and about parenthood. We are shown various different reactions by the boys in 4C and they learn different things …

(h) The ending of the novel is particularly important as we see Simon learning about himself and his feelings about his father and mother …

(i) The idea of 'The Quest for the Holy Grail' is important in the novel and is related to the theme of education …

(j) Overall, therefore, Anne Fine explores the reality of many teenagers' experience of school. She shows some who resist the systems of school life and others who do not. She shows how school is not just about academic lessons but also about growing up and understanding oneself. My opinion of the book was …

Simon's relationships

Look at the passage beginning 'I'm going mad' on page 133 and ending 'the stream of cars slowing unwillingly for the roundabout' on page 138. Then answer questions from page 196 to page 198.

Word

1. Consider the following words used in this chapter using *ie* and *ei*.

- Write in the appropriate combination of vowels:

  believe   friend
  receive   impatient
  fiercest   experience

- What is the general rule that you can use to help you remember when to use which combination of letters?

2. Look at the following sentences where a word is made up of a verb plus a suffix, to make a noun.

(a) He could have pointed out that any rainwater that fell on the flour baby might clean her up a bit or make up some weight from the *leakage*.

verb = to leak   suffix = age   noun = leakage

(b) As had been proved more than once on the football field, dogged determination was one of Wayne's most salient characteristics.

verb = to determine   suffix = ation   noun = determination

- Look at the list of words and suffixes below. See if you can link each word with a suffix, to change its meaning, and write it in column 3
- In the fourth column write whether the word has turned into a noun, verb or adjective

word	suffix	new word	type
mile	ful		
achieve	al		
wast(e)	age		
refus(e)	ment		
slav(e)	ist		
parent	ery		
fatal	ship		
friend	ful		
care	er		
book	hood		
sing	ful		
colour	let		

Sentence

Look at the conversation between Simon and his mother beginning 'I'm going mad' and ending 'Bye mum' (page 134). The interchange reveals a lot about Simon's mother's character and her relationship with her son.

Imagine she is writing a diary entry about what happened with Simon this morning. Write down her thoughts and feelings about the conversation. Focus on transforming the direct speech that Anne Fine gives us, into reported speech. An example of this is given in the second sentence below:

It was another strange morning today with Simon. He came into the kitchen and told me that he was going insane. I jokingly told him to be nice to Hyacinth as she might help him out, only to be scowled at horribly. I really don't know what's the matter with him at the moment.

Text

1. Re-read the section from 'This is your fault' (page 133) to 'the stream of cars slowing unwillingly for the roundabout (page 138).'

- Underline all the active verbs in the paragraph.
- In groups of four agree on the following roles: director, Simon, Mum and Wayne.
- Following the text carefully, dramatise the actions of the section using the dialogue given to you in the text.
- The director's role is to guide the actors in positioning and actions. Look carefully at the verbs to help you see where an action is needed.
- You may like to learn your lines. Then perform your scene to the class.

  Notice how much shorter it becomes in drama, once Simon's thoughts and observations are taken out of the text.

Getting into trouble

Look at the passage beginning 'With authority gone, the pack instantly went after their true quarry' on page 168 and ending 'Monday week, then' on page 178.

Word

Read over the passage below:

The flour baby _____ out and sailed over the energetically fighting scrum. She _____ high over the abandoned desks. Simon _____ beneath, tracking her flight, and managed to _____ her, puffing flour from every pore, just as Mr Cartright _____ to fetch his cigarettes...Without thinking twice, Simon _____ round and _____her in the air, giving himself enough time to _____ on the seat of a chair. _____ her safely, and _____ her out of Wayne's reach ...

In a rush of exhilaration, Simon suddenly astonished everyone around him by _____for the door. The noise was tremendous. From desk to desk he _____, leaving wobbly wooden legs _____ frantically, and chairs _____ over backwards. He _____ the flour baby high, and, as he jumped, what Mr Cartright said _____ in his ears. 'Do you want to know your problem, Simon Martin? You sell yourself too short.' He _____ from Wayne's desk to Russ's in a clatter of flying pens and rulers. He _____ Philip Brewster's calculator flying. He _____ over Luis's desk entirely. And with one last tremendous bound, he _____ to safety. He was through the door, _____ the air with a fist ...

- Insert verbs to create a sense of energy as Simon tries to rescue his flour baby and then escape from the class. You may want to use a book or electronic thesaurus to help you find a variety of exciting and appropriate verbs.
- Underline the prepositions.
- When you have finished, compare your verbs with Anne Fine's (page 169). Think about which words create the best sense of power and movement.

Sentence

Re-read page 168 from 'With authority gone, the pack instantly went after their true quarry' to page 174, 'Just set the things out to look interesting, and write a label explaining what they are.'

Anne Fine creates excitement for the reader in this passage by her choice of vocabulary and also the structure of the section. She builds it up by describing how Simon feels confident and exhilarated at the beginning of the passage and then uses bathos by showing how everything goes wrong from then on.

- Select a line that shows how confident Simon begins to feel.
- Can you identify the line where things begin to go wrong?
- Select three sentences from the first four pages of this extract that portray Simon as pathetic, isolated and threatened.
- Select three sentences that suggest the rest of the class and the teachers as threatening and attacking. Comment on particular words and phrases that you think convey this well.

Text

1. Look at the passage beginning on page 173, and ending on page 176, 'In vain he waited for Simon to make a move' to 'Baroom! Baroom! Pow!' Look carefully at Anne Fine's paragraphing.

   Reasons to change to a new paragraph are as follows:
   - change of time or pause in time
   - change of place
   - new speaker
   - change of topic.

   Can you pinpoint the reason why she has chosen to change to each new paragraph? The first four in the passage are done for you.

   (a) Paragraph 1: Pause in time
   (b) Paragraph 2: New speaker – Mr Higham speaks

(c) Paragraph 3: New topic – Simon's response

(d) Paragraph 4: New speaker – Simon

2. Imagine that you are the headteacher at Simon's school. Despite the fact that he is our hero at the end of the book, his behaviour in the last chapter could not go unpunished in the school.

Write a formal letter from the headteacher, in response to complaints by Mr Higham and Mr Cartright and concerns from Miss Arnott, asking Simon's mother to come to the school for a meeting to discuss his behaviour. Remember to make up the school address, Mrs Martin's address and the date.

3. Improvise in a group the meeting between Simon, the headteacher, any teacher you feel appropriate and Mrs Martin.

Glossary

9   **riveting sight:** something that fixes your attention

        snaffled up the Boffins: took the cleverest

11   **mutinous wave:** noises of disagreement

14   **a lone reed over the silt of the rest:** like a single plant sticking out of the mud

        You're reaping as ye sowed: a phrase from the Bible suggesting the result you get depends on what you put into it

16   **Baudelaire:** Charles Baudelaire, a French poet (1812-67)

17   **patois:** a language or form of language particular to a group of people

19   **latent:** hidden

        maimed: crippled, disfigured

20   **prolonged riff of resentment:** repeated and lengthy moaning

        disgruntlement: disgust or disappointment

21   **memorandum:** written message

22   **supplanted:** replaced

25   **surreptitiously:** secretly

26   **reeling:** tottering, staggering

        sociopaths: people who behave in a thoughtless, often criminal way

27   **sincere quest for mathematical enlightenment**: a real desire to know the correct answer

        sheer rapture: utter delight

        beguiling: enchanting, attractive

29   **spurn:** reject

        Prudently: carefully and sensibly

30   **small gesture of defiance:** small action to defy against the teacher

        neanderthal: rough and clumsy, as early man would have been

30	**doused down:** quietened
31	**conciliatory fashion:** friendly way
32	**daunt:** frighten, discourage
	came up trumps: succeed in the game
33	**arcane and dubious gestures:** worrying movements and signals understood by few
	new-fangled philistinism: lack of concern today for education and culture
36	**fodder:** food
	fibroids: benign tumours
37	**frittering away:** waste
39	**taunted:** teased
40	**maltreatment:** ill-treatment
41	**woollies:** jumpers or cardigans
	trawl: run through
	pen runnel: the line at the top of traditional school desks where pens could lie
	assiduously: carefully
44	*salubrious*: healthy
	grazed his consciousness: entered his mind
45	**broody:** moody, wanting to have a baby
46	**Old Crone:** old witch
	middle-aged spread: putting on weight with age
50	**nark:** police informer
	stool pigeon: police informer
53	**a doddle:** easy to do
	cloth-eared: deaf
54	*retarded*: mentally backward
	fiendish: devilish, wicked
55	**Furtively:** secretly
	hoisting: pulling up
56	**meagre:** scimpy
57	**hoodlums:** rowdy children
58	**retinue:** line following behind him

118 **swathe of mayhem:** how much trouble he could create

pedagogic: teacher-like response

120 **corroboration:** supporting, backing up

adamant: stubbornly firm

121 **potential:** possible, would-be

engendered: started up

conspiratorially: plotting together

consternation: dismay

123 **pillorying:** ridiculing

124 **floored:** defeated, left not knowing what to do

125 **entrepreneurial:** the ability to think up ideas to make money in business

morosely: miserably

126 **pugilists:** fighters

129 *main:* sea

surreptitiously: secretly

131 **spontaneously:** without being asked

132 **elusive:** hard to find

133 **prodigious:** astonishing and large

demur: raise objections

134 **pass muster:** be acceptable

137 **litany:** list, spoken in a way that sounds like a prayer

138 **tenor:** a voice usually of an adult male, higher than a bass, which is able to sing the tune

139 **taking her look of temporary indecision for one of pitiful entreaty:** mistaking her thoughtful look as one desperately signalling for help

140 **horse sense:** common sense

141 **salient:** clear, most striking

The Quest for the Holy Grail: a mythical journey made by knights to find the cup Christ was said to have drunk from before he was crucified. It stands for the most important search in life

184 **blizzard:** snow storm
185 **rills and rivulets:** small rivers
petty: unimportant
ill-gotten gains: money collected unfairly
186 **sou'wester:** wind from the south west
valour: bravery
187 **unfettered:** not held back or restrained

Title list

Post-1914 Fiction

0 582 43446 7	I'm the King of the Castle	Susan Hill
0 582 02660 1	The Woman in Black	Susan Hill
0 582 06016 8	Brave New World	Aldous Huxley
0 582 06017 6	The Cone-Gatherers	Robin Jenkins
0 582 08174 2	Picnic at Hanging Rock	Joan Lindsay
0 582 06557 7	Lamb	Bernard MacLaverty
0 582 44722 4	Chinese Cinderella	Adeline Yen Mah
0 582 28732 4	Fiela's Child	Dalene Matthee
0 582 08170 X	Lies of Silence	Brian Moore
0 582 43447 5	Animal Farm	George Orwell
0 582 06023 0	The Great Gatsby	F Scott Fitzgerald
0 582 46146 4	Of Mice and Men	John Steinbeck
0 582 82764 7	Of Mice and Men plain edition	John Steinbeck
0 582 46148 0	The Red Pony	John Steinbeck
0 582 46147 2	The Pearl	John Steinbeck
0 582 46149 9	The Moon is Down	John Steinbeck
0 582 46150 2	Tortilla Flat	John Steinbeck
0 582 461510	Cannery Row	John Steinbeck
0 582 46152 9	East of Eden	John Steinbeck
0 582 46153 7	The Grapes of Wrath	John Steinbeck
0 582 43448 3	Daz 4 Zoe	Robert Swindells
0 582 44737 2	Dosh	Robert Swindells

Short story collections

0 582 43453 X	A Northern Childhood
0 582 42943 9	Myths and Legends
0 582 48852 4	Survivors
0 582 43454 8	Twisters
0 582 48850 8	Different Cultures
0 582 28730 8	Quartet of Stories
0 582 23369 0	The Human Element & Other Stories
0 582 43449 1	A Roald Dahl Selection
0 582 28931 9	Stories Old and New
0 582 03922 3	Stories from Asia
0 582 28928 9	Mystery and Horror
0 582 02661 X	Ghost Stories
0 582 28929 7	Global Tales
0 582 29249 2	Ten D H Lawrence Short Stories
0 582 48852 4	Seize the Fire

Post-1914 Poetry

0 582 29248 4	Voices of the Great War
0 582 35149 9	Poetry 1900 to 1975
0 582 25401 9	Poems 2

Post-1914 Plays

0 582 30242 0	Absent Friends	Alan Ayckbourn
0 582 43450 5	Mirad, a Boy from Bosnia	Ad de Bont
0 582 06019 2	The Winslow Boy	Terrence Rattigan
0 582 22389 X	P'Tang, Yang, Kipperbang & other TV plays	Jack Rosenthal
0 582 43445 9	Educating Rita	Willy Russell
0 582 08173 4	Shirley Valentine	Willy Russell
0 582 25383 7	Ten Short Plays	
0 582 06014 1	The Royal Hunt of the Sun	Peter Shaffer
0 582 09712 6	Equus	Peter Shaffer
0 582 06015 X	Pygmalion	Bernard Shaw
0 582 07786 9	Saint Joan	Bernard Shaw
0 582 25396 9	The Rivals/The School for Scandal	Richard Brinsley Sheridan

Post-1914 Stories from Different Cultures

0 582 48850 8	Different Cultures	
0 582 28730 8	Quartet of Stories	
0 582 06011 7	July's People	Nadine Gordimer
0 582 25398 5	Heat and Dust	Ruth Prawer Jhabvala
0 582 07787 7	Cry, the Beloved Country	Alan Paton
0 582 03922 3	Stories from Asia	
0 582 28929 7	Global Tales	
0 582 78627 4	Summer Lightning and other Short Stories	Olive Senior
0 582 64264 7	The Lonely Londoners	Sam Selvon
0 582 23699 1	Sozaboy	Ken Saro-Wiwa
0 582 64265 5	A Brighter Sun	Sam Selvon
0 582 26455 3	Scarlet Song	Mariama Ba
0 582 64231 0	Dragon Can't Dance	E Lovelace
0 582 78619 3	The Jumbie Bird	I Khan
0 582 78633 9	Old Story Time and Smile Orange	Trevor Rhone
0 582 27602 0	Dilemma of a Ghost and Anowa	Ama Ata Aidou
0 582 78620 7	Plays for Today	D Walcott, D Scott, E Hill
0 582 64267 1	In the Castle of my Skin	George Lamming

Post-1914 Non-Fiction

0 582 25391 8	Genres
0 582 25384 5	Diaries and Letters
0 582 28932 7	Introducing Media
0 582 25386 1	Travel Writing
0 582 08837 2	Autobiographies
0 582 01736 X	The Diary of Anne Frank

Pre-1914 Fiction

0 582 07720 6	Pride and Prejudice	Jane Austen
0 582 07719 2	Jane Eyre	Charlotte Brontë
0 582 07782 6	Wuthering Heights	Emily Brontë
0 582 07783 4	Great Expectations	Charles Dickens
0 582 42944 7	Oliver Twist	Charles Dickens
0 582 23664 9	A Christmas Carol	Charles Dickens
0 582 23662 2	Silas Marner	George Eliot
0 582 07788 5	Far from the Madding Crowd	Thomas Hardy

Pre-1914 Collections

0 582 28931 9	Stories Old and New
0 582 25384 5	Diaries and Letters
0 582 25386 1	Travel Writing
0 582 33807 7	19th Century Short Stories of Mystery and Passion
0 582 48852 4	Seize the Fire

Pre-1914 Poetry

0 582 22585 X	Poems from Other Centuries

Pre-1914 Plays

0 582 25397 7	She Stoops to Conquer	Oliver Goldsmith
0 582 24948 1	Three Plays	Henrik Ibsen
0 582 25408 6	Volpone	Ben Jonson
0 582 81708 3	Doctor Faustus (A text)	Christopher Marlowe
0 582 25409 4	Doctor Faustus (B text)	Christopher Marlowe
0 582 28930 0	Starting Shakespeare	
0 582 43444 0	The Devil's Disciple	Bernard Shaw
0 582 07785 0	Arms and the Man	Bernard Shaw
0 582 28731 6	The Duchess of Malfi	John Webster
0 582 07784 2	The Importance of Being Earnest	Oscar Wilde

Pre-1914 Non-Fiction

0 582 26475 8	Sundiata, an Epic of Old Mali	D T Niane
0 582 26473 1	The Life of Olaudah Equiano	Edited by Paul Edwards